Hysteria 3

Winning Stories, Poems and Flash Fiction from Hysteria 2014 Writing
Competition
by
The Hysterectomy Association.

Edited by Linda Parkinson-Hardman.

Hysteria 3

Published by: The Hysterectomy Association
ISBN: 978-0-9927429-4-2

A catalogue record for this book is available from The British Library.

Telephone: 0843 289 2142
Website: www.hysterectomy-association.org.uk

All characters in this publication are fictitious and any resemblance to real persons, living or dead is purely coincidental.

Cover Image: © Michalbellan | Dreamstime.com – Fresh Lemon Drop In The Water

About the Hysteria Writing Competition

Hysteria is an annual writing competition for women only; it opens on the 1st April each year and closes at midnight on the 31st August. You can find out more on the Hysterectomy Association website about the next competition at: hysterectomy-association.org.uk/hysteria-writing-competition/.

Acknowledgements

The competition and this anthology wouldn't have been possible without the support and help of everyone that took part and the judges who gave their time.

This book is dedicated to them and to the users of the Hysterectomy Association.
Thank you. Linda Parkinson-Hardman (editor).

Judges

Abigail Wyatt, Amanda Quinn, Sarah Hegarty (Past Winner), Sophie Duffy, Tracy Fells (Past Winner) and Veronica Bright. Our judges have each contributed to the anthology by sharing their advice to entrants. You can find their thoughts, together with some from last year's judges in the final section of the anthology.

Writer in Residence

This was the first year we introduced a Writer in Residence for the writing competition. Thanks go to Bridget Whelan for taking on this role.

You can find Bridget's pearls of writing wisdom on the website here: hysterectomy-association.org.uk/author/bridgetwhelan/

Contents

Foreword

For the last three years, I've been in the privileged position of being able to read a multitude of entries to the Hysteria Writing Competition. With every one I'm impressed by the ability of their creators to come up with different ways of expressing age-old experiences. Each one shines a slightly different light on the constantly recurring themes which resonate within women's lives. This year has been no exception.

For the first time we introduced a new category to the competition, Flash Fiction. It takes real skill to condense a complete story into just 250 words and make it meaningful and enjoyable for the reader. I am really pleased to say that the success of this category means it will definitely continue in future years.

We also reinstated the poetry category and again, the exceptionally high standard of all the entries means that Hysteria will continue the poetry section too.

Finally, for the first time I'm pleased to have some wonderful advice from this year's judges and a few of previous year's judges. For those who weren't successful this time around and for those who would like to enter in the future, the advice makes great reading.

Linda Parkinson-Hardman (Editor)

Flash Fiction

The Flash Fiction category was open to entries with a maximum word count of 250 words. These ultra-short stories needed to be complete and give the reader the satisfaction of not being left hanging.

The challenge when writing flash fiction is to tell a complete story in which every word is essential. It's important that the writer pares down the padding, peels away the layers and ends up with the pure essence of the story.

A Brief History of Cycling – Helen Chambers

I watched the confident children cycling with envious eyes. Later, alone, I scraped my shins on a borrowed bike. Disappointing.

Small 'stabiliser' wheels not very stable; too small and high up. Dad jogging behind me, holding the saddle, suddenly not there. Pavement slipping by. Wind flattening my hair, tears stinging my eyes and I'm doing it!

Freedom!

Glory!

Success!

Showing off. One hand off the handlebars. Two hands off. Slow-motion tumbling. Scrapes, cuts, bruised pride. More careful.

Cycling in Suffolk. Others coasting up and sailing down the hills, using gears. Effortless. Pedalling frantically to keep up, heart pounding and throat dry.

Savings squandered. Forest-green bike with gears. Beautiful. I'll grow into it. Cycling Proficiency at school; seat too high, won't lower. Wobbling on corners. Scraped through the test.

Old-fashioned basket for Christmas. Wanted modern plastic one like friends. Didn't hide disappointment.

Cycling everywhere – bike tours after exams. Scraped through exams. Glory and freedom on bike tour! Forest-green bike (with wicker basket) taken on train to University. Iconic. Cycling everywhere. Glory and freedom!

Stolen. Never recovered. Deeply disappointing.

Cheap replacement bike. Plastic basket. Never stolen, though always left unlocked. Disappointing.

Attaching child seats, tag-alongs. Watching my children learn. Success! Glory! Freedom! Wind in their hair, tears in their eyes and mine.

Off-road cycling on new bike. Plastic basket and fifteen gears. (Seeking wicker basket.) Scraped by brambles, stung by nettles. Freedom!

Chasing grown-up children, pedalling frantically to keep up. Throat dry. No scrapes.

Freedom.

Still glorious!

Helen Chambers lives in a riverside village in North East Essex, with her husband and two nearly-grown up children, where she is involved in two writer's groups. Many artists and creative people live here too, giving her no end of inspiration and writing material! She is currently studying for an MA in Creative Writing at the University of Essex, where her 50-second play 'Revolution' was recently performed as part of Essex's Fiftieth Anniversary celebrations. She also teaches in a local primary school, particularly relishing drama and music activities, as well as teaching writing and motivating reading. She enjoys writing short stories, flash fiction and drama (including radio drama); and she was shortlisted in November 2014 for the 'Big Picture Competition' (SaveAs Writers).

Website: about.me/helen_chambers

Glory Hole – Trish Leake

We're in a dark, damp, cold place – the glory hole. Sunday afternoons are spent round at my Granny's house, we kids are sent downstairs so that the grownups can talk. Careful on the steep concrete steps, past the coal hole, my sister, my older cousins Sarah and Robert. It smells musty, hard to breathe. There are three rooms: one central one, a side one where Aunt Sadie hangs out ghost-sheets, and a long room full of tools. We're not allowed in there but Robert always disappears, poking about. The bare light bulb, dim and low, makes the corners and walls even darker.

I am six, my sister's nine and Sarah's seventeen and going out with Ed, her steady boyfriend. Saturday nights they go to the cinema and Sunday afternoons, down in the cellar, she tells us every last detail. Robert frequently springs out or clangs a tool. We jump a mile and squeal.

She's in the middle of 'The Blob' and I'm holding my breath. It is relentless. I can see the green, glowing, formless monster advancing, squelching, and consuming everything it can reach.

Robert slurps wetly on my shoulder. He has crept in on purpose.

I scream all the way up the steps to the hallway, yelling for my mother. Next week it's 'Bride of Frankenstein'.

Trish Leake. My working history is in libraries and tefl teaching. After a stroke at 50, I ended up in Devon with more time on my hands to take my prior scribbling more seriously.

I write poetry and am halfway through a novel. I also am writing about lives of my historical female family members, 'cos if I don't write them down they'll be lost with my mum, and she's ninety-four!

But my best love is flash fiction...the paring down of language and making every word count. 'Glory Hole' is a childhood memory - we've all got them, so get writing!

A Day or Two – Diane Simmons

The lock to the hen coop is broken. Most of his hens have stayed put, but Tom can't see Gracie. Gorgeous Gracie, his favourite. Swearing, he secures the fence and searches again. Nothing.

'Bloody buggering vandals!' he shouts to his wife as he marches in their back door. 'All this time I've spent protecting them from foxes and some moron's broken in and taken Gracie. Of all the hens ...'

'Oh, Tom, no! And on top of your best layer dying too ...'

'I can't take much more of this. The work I've put into them since I retired ...'

'I know.' Susan puts down her knitting and hugs him. 'Would you like a cup of tea?'

'No I don't want tea – I'm off to ring the police.'

Susan starts knitting again, thinks about all the lovely eggs his hens have given them. They're very creamy, but not really worth all the time he spends fretting, or the hours researching he does. And they're certainly not worth missing out on holidays for because he's too neurotic to leave them. It's time he found a new hobby. Bridge would be perfect – something to get him out for a few hours without it taking over his whole life. She'll suggest it in a day or two.

Remembering his stricken face, she takes the bolt cutters out of her handbag and smiles. A day or two should be just right. And if he needs more persuading, she can always help things along.

A Delicate Operation – Diane Simmons

Jeanette and Alison sit in a huddle in the playground playing with Alison's new doctor's bag. Jeanette's been all over her since she got it. Even though I'm not sure I've got my facts quite right, I decide to try and get Alison's attention. I saunter past them, announce loudly, 'Ma mum's had the tops of her toes cut off!'

Jeanette looks up, sneers. 'Aye, right.'

'She has! They cut out the middle bits and put the tops back on. That's why I had school dinners last week!'

'Prove it,' Jeanette says.

***

When I arrive at school the next day, Jeanette and Alison are there, waiting, sniggering. Jeanette shouts out, 'Have you got your mum's toes in your bag?' I meet her stare and reach into my schoolbag.

'These went through her toes after they'd chopped them,' I say, as I pull out two long needles. Alison peers at them, but Jeanette screams and legs it.

'Whit're you screaming for?' Alison shouts over to her. 'There's no' even any blood on them, stupit!'

'There's tons on the corks though,' I say. 'The ones the doctors put on the ends.'

Alison grins. 'Is there? Are they in your bag? Can I see?'

'Ma mum keeps them on the mantelpiece. Come round after school if you want.'

She takes my arm and as we swagger past Jeanette, Alison smiles at me. 'Shall we play doctors at playtime, Maggie?' She darts a look at Jeanette. 'There's no' everybody that's cut out for medicine!'

Diane Simmons. Forced to give up work due to arthritis, Diane started writing seven years ago when she studied Creative Writing with The OU. Her short stories and flash fiction have won or been placed in many competitions including *Woman and Home, SHE/This Morning, Writers' Forum,* Worcester Litfest, Ink Tears, 99 Fiction and The Frome Festival, as well as being short listed and long listed numerous times. She has been published recently in *Mslexia, Scraps, Eating my Words, Flashes of Fiction, Five Stop Story, FlashFlood, The Yellow Room and Fifty Flashes of Fiction.*

Having recently overcome her fear of reading out loud, she was thrilled to be asked to perform some of her flash fiction at the 2014 National Flash Fiction Day event in Bristol and very nearly enjoyed doing it.

Diane is the mother of three grown up and nearly financially independent children and lives in Bath with her husband, Phil.

A Husband's Loss – Maureen Bennie

The gold locket hangs like a free pendulum from his shaky gnarled hand. The fine chain wrapped around his arthritic knuckles. Occasionally, his rheumy eyes drift to the inscription, caught every so often, by flames from the firelight.

Still in his funeral suit from yesterday, he sits in her armchair where she had knitted the family countless oversized jumpers. Photos of the grandchildren smile and laugh on the sideboard, amidst the many condolence cards and withered poinsettia. Her favourite radio station plays this morning's drama on the dusty 'Bush' radio.

Not hearing the voices, his thoughts are with her. Tears run over hollow cheeks and through day old, silver stubble as he glances the 'Alternative Therapist' business card on the table next to the herbal medicine in the chocolate-brown bottle.

They had tried everything. All the treatments the doctors had recommended and every natural path. The brand new laptop in its case, sits propped against the chair. A tool to seek specialists in the field, support groups and remedies. Finally used to convey the heart breaking outcome to her many friends, from her bountiful past.

Warmed by the fire he closes his weary eyes. Drifting memories. Her sparkling presence every time she entered a room. The smile that opened people's hearts. That soft loving kiss.

Sleep swathes him. Numbing the pain that snuffed the light.

His eyelids flicker. She's with him, holding his hand. Ethereal, her body embraces him with her loneliness. They are together once more.

Maureen Bennie. My name is Maureen, generally known as Mo. I live in picturesque Bradford on Avon with my teenage son. Having moved here ten years ago, I initially ran my own café (Granny Mo's) for three years but now work from home buying and selling vintage goods. Currently studying for an Open Degree with the OU, I hope to achieve a B.A.Hons in a couple of years. I have two elder children and three little folk as I call them, my grandchildren. All of whom live in Cornwall, from where I originally hail from.

I have taken to writing later in life, having always felt the yearning but never had the time. My ambition, is to have one of my novels published that I am presently working on, or indeed all three! 'A Husband's Loss' is my first publication. A first significant and inspiring step towards my goal.

Website: grannydotsemporium.co.uk

A Lust for Blood – Alison Wassell

'Tell me about yourself,' he asks her cleavage. She knows she has only two minutes. She hates speed dating, but her best friend has dragged her here. She may as well have some fun.

'I'm a butcher,' she says. The corners of his mouth twitch into a smile as he waits for confirmation that she is joking. She silently returns the smile. He squanders his half of the conversation, swallowing several times before finding his voice. His eyes remain fixed on her breasts.

'Do you need many qualifications for that?' he says, at last. Not really, she tells him. A strong stomach, a lust for blood and a sharp set of knives are the only things that are required. She thinks for a second.

'And a decent knowledge of anatomy,' she adds. She considers telling him what cut of meat he is currently staring at. She decides against it. There are beads of perspiration on his forehead. She leans forward slightly, encouraging him to speak.

He clears his throat; asks if she enjoys her work. Her smile is genuine now. In what other job, she asks, could she dismember corpses with no questions asked? He takes a long drink from his glass.

'Serial killer?' he offers. She warms to him, slightly. She likes them with a sense of humour. She beckons him closer, as though she is about to divulge a secret. She imagines his salty taste.

'Yes,' she whispers, as the bell rings.

'There is always that.'

Alison Wassell is a former primary school teacher. She volunteers in a charity shop and pays her bills by selling bottled gas part-time in her family's business whilst attempting to become a 'proper' writer. This is the only real ambition she has ever had.

She has been longlisted, shortlisted and placed in numerous competitions and published in a handful of anthologies, including **Hysteria 1.** She has most recently been published in the anthology **My Baby Shot Me Down** (Blinding Books 2014). She doesn't really want to be a novelist, and wishes people would have more respect for short stories and flash fiction. She fantasizes about one day earning a living from her writing.

Alison shares her home with her cat, Lily, who remains unimpressed by her achievements. When she grows up, she wants to be Alice Munro.

Blog: alisoninwriterland.blogspot.co.uk/

A Perfect Blend of Sweet and Sour – Christine Griffin

Saturday

5pm

You're planning Beef Wellington for the main course with baby seasonal vegetables. You've splashed out on a good Burgundy and when he's finished all that he'll be nice and mellow.. Then your party piece – Rhubarb Fool. A perfect blend of sweet and sour. Coffee and mints to follow. Maybe a brandy. And if he can manage anything else, he'll be eating out of the palm of your hand.

10 pm

You load the cold Beef Wellington into the car along with the limp baby seasonal vegetables and the slightly soggy Rhubarb Fool. You decant the claret to drink later, and put the bottle in the boot. His letter box is stiff but you force the Beef Wellington and the vegetables through and they land with a satisfying plop on his prize Persian rug. You can't help hearing the peal of girly laughter from upstairs.

The bottle breaks easily and the shards sit nicely under the tyres of his Mercedes. Now what to do with the Rhubarb Fool? It's then you realise you haven't eaten a thing. Half an hour in the fridge while you eat the fish and chips you buy on the way home and it'll be perfect.

Who says you shouldn't drink red wine with fish? Or eat chips with your fingers? You've never enjoyed anything as much in your whole life. Half an hour later you're licking the Rhubarb Fool bowl clean. Delicious.

A perfect blend of sweet and sour.

Christine Griffin. Since retirement, Christine has immersed herself in all forms of writing and is a member of various local writing groups which have provided her with many exciting ideas and much stimulus. She has been successful in local and national competitions and has had work published in several anthologies. Her stories and poems have been featured at live fiction events and also on local radio. Her latest success was performing her work at the Cheltenham Literature Festival. She has also had two short plays performed locally.

The featured piece 'A Perfect Blend of Sweet and Sour' arose from a writing assignment at Cheltenham Writers' Circle entitled 'Memorable Meals'. Christine would love to write a novel but knows in her heart of hearts that she doesn't have the stamina! So on with the short story – her favourite form.

A Sleeping Beauty – Elizabeth Heasman

Dave Charming sat awkwardly sipping banana daiquiri. Cajoled into speed dating Friday at The Castle, the gallant knight had to get back on his horse. His last girlfriend was an evil witch. It transpired she'd been letting her hair down with several fellas.

He watched beauty move around the tables, glass of prosecco in hand, seemingly asleep smiling vacantly to her suitors. Crudely cackling inebriated ugliness assembled until beauty finally came before him.

Unable to resist Dave gently kissed beauty's delicate hand, awakening dazzling eyes. Holding hands they headed for the bar. Dragons' slayed Charming had found his true love.

Elizabeth Heasman (Lizzie) was born in 1970 and is married to Malcolm. They have two grown up children, Jacob and Charity. The benefits to living in the rural area of Lewes, East Sussex are thoroughly enjoyed by their extended furry family of three giddy dogs and more sober elderly cat.

Following a career largely in legal and financial administration and retail, Lizzie's world of writing was re-opened after attending a creative writing class at a local college. After completing the follow-up course she now attends an on-going weekly writer's class, 'Penwalkers' in Brighton.

Lizzie admits she loves learning new things and has attended several classes over the decades, from sewing to achieving Associate level with ILEX. But Lizzie's biggest buzz has been discovering a passion for flash fiction. She finds it fascinating. To be able to construct and convey a complete story with just a few words sparks boundless possibilities for expression. Website: lizzieheasman.com

A Wonderful Life – Gayle Letherby

Conceived in love the child is born a beauty, healthy and strong. Quick to smile she sleeps through the night and is record breaking in toddler milestones.

School and university days are happy; as popular as she is clever, as artistic as she is athletic, success is achieved across the board.

Following one or two semi-serious relationships - all learning experiences - she meets her soul mate and marries (a little earlier than her peers) in the same year as her promotion to partner (much earlier than anyone in the history of the firm).

Babies follow and the family years are full of laughter and fun, of holidays in the sunshine and more certificates than the walls of their beautiful home can take.

The children leave; happy partnerships and good jobs secured. Alone with her partner (both in name and experience) their mother does not suffer any empty nest symptoms. Applauded for her charity work, well known in the community and beyond; an accolade from the reigning monarch the crowning glory to a glittering career.

Retirement is full, supported by well-earned pensions and a not so small lottery win. After ten happy years her husband dies in his sleep. For almost another decade she continues as doting grandmother and faithful friend. Content with her lot she too dies gently.

***

A familiar ache and tugging feeling disturbs my daydream. My knickers are wet, there is blood. Dreams of my child's wonderful life dashed for another month.

Gayle Letherby. I am a sociologist, a civil celebrant and a writer of both fiction and non-fiction. Much of my academic and other writing has been stimulated by my own experiences and interests, as is the piece published in this anthology.

I am particularly concerned with the complex material and emotional lives we all have and in identity and relationships. I have recently begun to blog about some of my professional and personal interests and views. If interested please go to Arwenack Celebrants (arwenack.co.uk).

Adrift – Sade' Norwood

She flew a thousand miles to find herself, but as she stood on the tarmac she felt even more lost.

They all had stories and jokes of the Mother she never knew and even though she came there for exactly that, it made her resent her even more. She was enraged with envy that they had the chance to know her, to hold her, to laugh with her, to cry with her, to have fun with her, or to just have a conversation.

She thought that this would give her closure but it made Pandoras box even larger. As she exited the airport, she realized she hadn't found herself at all, but had lost herself completely.

Sade' Norwood discovered her passion for short fiction in the Fifth Grade during a fourth quarter English assignment. As a child, one dreams of being many things; a doctor, fire fighter, astronaut, but during that assignment, Sade' was overcome with an intense joy that she had never felt. She knew she was born to be a writer. Virginia State University was where Sade' focused on enhancing her creative talents. She joined the fashion organization, TAMM (Textile Apparel Merchandising Management) where she assisted in the orchestration of two fashion shows and other fashion-related events. She became the President of the University's English Club and had the most enrolled members during her presidency.

Since graduation, Sade' has worked for Saks Fifth Avenue, Theory LLC, and Vince using her creative talents in various arenas. TheEnigmaticMind.com was launched early 2014 to introduce the world to Sade's creative writing talents.

Follow Sade' on Instagram : @__piecesofme_

Poetry

The poetry category sought entries which had a maximum of 20 lines, not including spaces. Many of our entries followed a strict rule of either four or five line stanzas, but a few challenged this convention.

Poetry is not something that can easily be defined; but it is a written form which lends itself to being spoken out loud. Sometimes, it is easier to understand poetry when you hear it, rather than read it because the rhythm and emphasis of the words can be more easily defined.

The poet's challenge is to create a strong visual image and emotional reaction in the reader or listener.

I Do Not Love You – Polly Hall

I do not love you as a practised speech or polished aria,
I do not love you as the crescendo of a soulful descant.
I love you as silence loves the space
between an exhalation and an inhalation -
as the eyelids of the opera singer gently close.

I love you as the printed quavers and minims
 on a stave wait to be given life
by an instrument or a voice.
Appassionato, con bravura; they don't matter.
I love you as the strings wait for a bow.

I love you as the pages of a book whisper apart
to awaken a much read passage.
I love you in the time it takes
my breath to dry this green ink;
I love you in the echo of your footsteps.

I love you in the repetition of our names, together -
the rolling of our consonants and vowels.
I love you because you really hear my music
and don't expect me to play it just for you.
You hear my music so I'll play it just for you.

Polly Hall. My background in holistic therapy and healing has given me a strong foundation in understanding the interconnectedness of life. I published my first non-fiction book, *The Art of Foot Reading*, in 2009. I'm rarely shocked by anything as I have such a vivid imagination. One of my favourite authors is Stephen King, he is a pure genius. That's not to say I try to write like him but I think you can learn a lot from successful writers.

I'm fascinated by people's motivations and backgrounds. I enjoy getting deep into the meaning of things and the minutiae. I am hoping that one day someone invents a machine that can record your dreams in multi-colour so you can play them back as a movie. I am currently studying an MA in Creative Writing at Bath Spa University and loving every minute of it. My main aim as a writer is to make the reader *feel* something whether that be a sense of dread or joy.

My blog - skywomb.blogspot.co.uk - was written as a creative response to my experience of hysterectomy. Twitter: @pollyfeet.

On the Point of Leaving for Pickering, Sometime In 1941 –

Janet Dean

Seeing me off at Doncaster,
tears at the brim,
not one dare
drop
on her Max Factored face.

Wearing Oxford bags,
coat collar up,
belt buckle trailing,
hands flitting
from pocket to glove.

Warm in the glow
of anticipation,
the steamy breath,
the act of departing.
I mouthed my goodbye,

waving to her.
She pushed her hand
through wavy hair,
not wanting
to wave back.

Market Day Blues – Janet Dean

Wednesday, first light; queuing
for Chelsea boots, green suede shoes.
Bristling for a bargain before school,

craving buttery leather,
stacked heels.

Disappointed, nothing fits.
Sachets of Inecto Hint of a Tint,
one Copper, one Chestnut,
brighten me up.

Saturday errands I run for you:
a slab of belly pork, a bag of biscuits, broken.
New tights, some black, some tan;
blobs of clear nail polish
control my runs.

Choosing buttons on the haberdasher's stall,
selecting the silver, picking at pearls,
allowing the black four-holes
to fall from my fingers.

Together, we go to buy the duvet and its blue cover,
days before I leave for college.

Janet Dean was born in Barnsley and now lives in York with her husband and two grown up children. She is finishing a long career in the public sector and preparing to write full time by studying part time for an MA in Creative Writing at York St John University.

As a poet she has been published in print and online magazines and anthologies, and was shortlisted in the Bridport Prize in 2012. Janet is currently working on a first collection and a novel. The resourcing and creation of identities is a theme which runs through her creative work. Find out more about Janet at deanknight.co.uk and read her blog at thepracticeofwating.blogspot.com

Cairo Chorus – Vicki Morley

Javelins of light slice the night sky.
The yellow glow slowly
approaches the city fringes
where huddled in rags,
workers sleep in the cemetery
below the Mokattam hills.

Mullahs, weary with arthritis,
climb endless stairs of stone
to switch on a
recording.

As the call to prayers
ricochets
across street canyons,
drones into cafes and shuttered windows,
the sound is echoed
by a canine chorus.
All the Cairo dogs tune up
for the day ahead.
They howl loud and long
to mourn the end of night.

Vicki Morley is a strange hybrid, having worked in intelligence at GCHQ and been head of two comprehensives she took early retirement and started writing short stories for her own enjoyment. Some of these were read at Falmouth's Telltales, a local writers' group. This was a useful antidote to removing slugs from the vegetable beds. Then she moved to the town of Penzance which is relatively slug free and she writes poems.

In 2014 she read a selection at Penzance's Golowan Festival and The Literary Festival. Her ambition is to keep the local independent bookshop open and is currently buying from their poetry selection.

DNA – Jayne Thickett

His heartbeat echoed mine,
each kick and turn tattooed my soul.

Came that rush of release and he found the breach,
to crest the waves of my agony, my labour of love.

Blue eyes searched for me
as he washed up on these strange, new shores. Outside.

I kissed his head, drank in his scent,
and would have tasted him if I could.

His breath was sweetest; his squalls swelled my heart
until that primal urge swallowed me whole.

They took him, too soon, to wash away the vernix;
to cleanse my womb from his skin.

But they cannot scrub away mitochondria.
He will always be of me. Mine.

Jayne Thickett is 41 years old. This is her first published poem, the other attempts are buried somewhere no one will ever find them. She has published several fiction pieces in print and around the net and once received an honourable mention from The Foundling Review. She continues to work on her novel when time and life allows.

She lives with her partner and son in Manchester, and also shares her home with an African Grey with an attitude problem, a Lhasa Apso who thinks he's a Rottweiler, and a catfish with nine lives. She is about to return to her old role of learning disability support worker after an eye-opening year as a hotel room attendant.

Le Castelat – Joy Blake

Packing up Le Castelat, again those boxes
I unhang the pictures, take down the tacks.
Sand crumbles in anthills on the floor,
books dust freckled, cards fall from
Bumpy walls along which I scratch
Nails like an emery board.

Pictures lining the floor like soldiers
Bali –back in the day, swapped
For a pair of jeans from the artist.
The Australian pair from aboriginal
cloth, kangaroo dreaming and goanna
packed in bubble wrap.

Japanese pen and ink sketches
in their frames, brush strokes contained.
Romeo and Juliet at the RSC in 1980
passion framed, is unhooked carefully
wrapped, although already cracked
our walls bared, the memories stacked.

Joy Blake has just given up full time English and Drama teaching to concentrate on writing, walking on the beach with her Westie and spending time with her first very active grandson.

She has been shortlisted twice for the Bridport prize, published in Hysteria in 2012 and has written freelance articles for a French/English magazine whilst living in France. She writes poetry, stories, flash fiction, bits of novels, many rants and is part of a writing group called Doppelgangers.

She has notebooks and memory sticks all over the place with unfinished, unedited pieces and is trying to unscramble these scraps to put together a pamphlet of poetry currently called 'Urban Coastal.' She loves just about everything she does, her family, travel and believes in Happiness by Design.

Kiss – Juliet Antill

(for Leah)

Fifteen years ago
I'm rolling like a barrel
of Best off a floor-bound mattress
three or four times
before morning.
My neighbour, five foot two
and skinny as a stray,
shouts from his door:
If it comes in t'night, duck, bang on t'wall.
(His wife is sour with rheumatics
and the wiping of skirting-boards.)
From my place on the floor
I rehearse the best point for my fist
as I wait – my whole body ready
for the great shucking out.
Now you deal the final kiss
to my cervix, for luck.

Juliet Antill. I live on the Isle of Mull with my two teenage daughters, where I teach mindfulness, stare at the hills and dance in my kitchen. I have had poems published in several magazines including Northwords Now and Poetry Scotland, and I won the Skye Reading Room's poetry competition earlier this year.

Website: julietantill.co.uk

Testing Time – Lucy Williams

A plastic stick lies in the bin, discarded by the dozen.
Sobriety will be a pleasure when you are ready to request it.
But for now I'm allowed a daily numbness,
while I'm mourning every lack of sickness.

Three laps of a clock, then I can search
for a life
line,
memorised instructions checked one last time.

Self-enforced showers wash away the minutes,
rubbing steamy glass to make view-holes.
I stare through, longing for a sense of blue,
then slow-motion towelling
as monthly windows are closed behind frosted glass.

Holding the cord in the bathroom,
I stare at the mirror to look at how I feel,
before returning to the tea, returning,
just me.

Lucy Williams has a BA Hons in Italian, a PG Dip in Translation Studies, and a Diploma in Commercial Authorship. She is currently studying Creative Writing with The Open University, and is particularly interested in travel writing, the translation of culturally-bound humour, crossing boundaries through Literature, and Creative Writing for therapeutic purposes.

After various roles in the Publishing Industry, Lucy now lives back in her hometown in Wales, where she works as an in-house Technical Author, and a freelance writer and translator, and once a month she can be found hosting her bookclub, 'Reading between the Wines' in her local pub.

Lucy recently became a Committee member of Honno Press, a volunteer-run Press in Abersytwyth, promoting Welsh Women's writing, and also works as a volunteer befriender with the National Autisitic Society, helping people with their communication skills through writing. Lucy has poetry published in *The Seventh Quarry* and *Roundyhouse* journals.

Follow Lucy on Twitter @lupes2, her blog theanarchiclout.wordpress.com and bookclub facebook.com/reading.wines.reading

A Mother Lets Go Again – Camilla Lambert

Throughout September while I slumped and slept
content for days to slide to weeks, a space
for thought to wane, hope to wax, time had crept,
marked by movements only I could trace,
soft flutters, flickers, kicks. Ambushed, caught,
all choice was taken from me. I woke
to sudden motherhood, and lay distraught
with emptiness, no child to soothe or stroke.

I watched them giving care that should be mine
to give. I was a cask which must contain
its tears, for, broken, could let loose malign
blight on his brittle life, and me to blame.
In double hurt, for memories long stored,
releasing him once more, I tear the cord.

November daffodils – Camilla Lambert

There must have been hundreds,
orange trumpets of celebration
arriving on our doorstep in November
to bring consolation, rays of light
to a dark tunnel I had never
known was there, thinking only
to move along well trodden tracks,
arriving on time at the station.

Instead I was stumbling, empty,
denied, tasting as never before fear's
salt flavour, prey to slippery guilt,
betrayed by an unknown disconnection,
buffeted by contrary gales of hope,

despair; in uncertain thrall
to our too early son, stick thin limbs,
no buttocks and ginger hair in curls.

Camilla Lambert moved to West Sussex two years ago, before that having lived on the Isle of Wight for over 18 years. It was there that she began to write poetry when she retired in 2007, seeking a total contrast from the life of a senior NHS manager.

She has had poems published in 'SOUTH', 'Interpreter's House' Sentinel Literary Quarterly and 'Poetry Cornwall', with a number being placed or highly commended in competitions. With another writing colleague, Ed Matyjaszek she edited an anthology of poems 'Island Voices', published in 2010.

In 2012 she gained an Open University First Class Honours degree in Literature with Creative Writing. She has also been involved in running writing competitions, and gets poetic sustenance from colleagues in several local writing groups. She is an active grandmother and gardener and escapes from time to time on walking holidays.

Short Stories

The short story category was for entries of up to 2,000 words, not including the title. The short story genre is a staple of writing competitions the world over and many writers will hone their skills in this medium before venturing into the world of longer fiction.

In some ways, writing short fiction is much harder than writing longer pieces, this is because the writer doesn't have the luxury of space and time to expand on a theme or introduce too many layers. Most short stories seem to work best when they consider a single perspective or a specific event.

Drowning in Lemon Juice – Tracey Glasspool

"You've cut your hair."

The words are out before I can stop them, but it's a shock – her hair was always so long. She lifts her hand, tucks a stray lock behind one ear; self-conscious.

"It looks good," I say. Her features are so delicate – the short cut should make her look younger, more vulnerable than she already is, but somehow it doesn't.

She doesn't smile. "He liked it long."

***

She comes in to the living room and we stand for a moment, both of us slightly lost.

"I've got your room ready," I say, trying to fill the silence. "The bed's all made and I've cleared the cupboards for you." Then I notice she doesn't have anything with her – no suitcase, no holdall. Nothing but a carrier bag. She sees me looking; reads the question on my face.

"I've left it all behind. There's nothing I want."

I scout around for something else to talk about. I can't believe I'm this dumbstruck with my own daughter. We should be chatting away non-stop like we used to. 'A couple of noisy magpies' my Alan used to say.

Then I hit on something – a reminder of better times. "Pancakes," I say. "Let's have pancakes, Lucy."

We used to have pancakes at least once a week, not just for Shrove Tuesday like everyone else. Lucy would have eaten them for breakfast,

42

lunch and dinner if I'd let her. Drowning in lemon juice and sparkling with sugar – I can almost smell them.

She hesitates.

Please, I'm willing her. Please say yes.

"Not now," she says, voice a whisper. "I think I'll just have a lie down."

And she's gone.

My throat feels thick; heavy and aching. One more thing he's taken from us.

***

Lucy's with her counsellor. I'm in a department store cafe just down the road, picking at a slice of fruitcake. It's like trying to swallow ashes.

I wish I could be in there with her, wish I could hear what they are saying. It should be me she's talking to.

"It's like with your writing," she said after her first session. "You always said you couldn't write at all if you thought someone would read your first draft. All that stuff that just flows out before you have a chance to shape it and mould it. That's how it is for me." And then she looked at me and her voice was so small, so despairing that it broke my already broken heart all over again. "I have to tell someone, mum."

But that someone's not me. I only get the edited version. I understand, I really do. But I'm still her mother; it still hurts.

***

We get through each day in our way and I start to think we're doing okay. That we are getting, well not over it, but getting on with it –

moving on as they say. Then this morning I reached out to her, just to touch her arm, and she flinched away from me as if I was about to strike her. I saw the shock on her face as soon as she realised what she'd done. I'm sure it was a mirror of my own face. We carried on, as if nothing had happened, but I dropped my hand. And later on, when she was in the garden, I went upstairs and I screamed into my pillow. Can I never reach out to my child again? Has he taken that too?

I'm in the department store, another day, another slice of cake. I'm watching two women; they're laughing together, joking. They must be a mother and daughter – they're different but the same if you know what I mean. Different hair colour, different build, different faces. But something about their expressions, the way they move and interact makes it obvious they share blood. Like my Lucy and me.

I want to go over to them. 'Make sure you notice,' I want to scream at the mother. 'Make sure you notice when something is wrong with her. Trust your instincts, always. Don't you ever find yourself in my position - wondering how the hell you could have missed the pain she was in.'

Because that's what people think, I know. I know how their whispers go. How could she not realise? How could she not see what was happening to her daughter? But I didn't. I really didn't.

***

I have my own counsellor now. He tells me it's not my fault. He tells me about the abusers – how clever they are, so charming and believable, in complete control at all times. And he tells me how clever the abused are too – so careful to hide any evidence, to conjure up the perfect excuse for a missed engagement or the too-long sleeves on a too-hot day. He tries to take away my guilt and my shame, but he can't. I'm terrified that I've lost her; that she's gone for good - that little girl and her dreams of being a doctor, or an astronaut, or a mermaid; that stroppy teenager with her outspoken views and her rebellion against the world; the young woman she became with her passion and her commitment and her beautiful soul.

My daughter. My blood. It was my job to notice.

It's a glorious day – travel brochure skies. I feel trapped in the house, restless. I can't breathe.

"How about a day at the beach?" I say.

She shakes her head, but I'm insistent. I need to get out. She needs to get out. In the end she just gives in and I feel a pang of guilt. Am I controlling her too?

We park, gather our bags, head for the sand. We spread towels, cast off shoes. I slip my t-shirt over my head and shimmy out of my jeans but Lucy stays as she is. She rolls up her trouser legs but her shirt sleeves remain down, the buttons fastened.

"It's so hot, Lucy," I say. "Why don't you go in for a swim?" But she shakes her head. I decide not to push anymore. Maybe it's enough that I got her here.

The water is too inviting and I dive in – the cold shock wonderful as I slide under. It's so calm beneath the surface, so tranquil. I wish I could stay here. It's like my problems are removed from me - part of another world, above my green and hazy cocoon. I feel like I'm drowning anyway, easier really just to stay.

But I can't of course. There are things I must face.

I resurface, take a gasp of air, look for Lucy. She's huddled up, arms wrapped tightly around her knees, staring into the distance. My long-ago mermaid would have been with me in the water, or dancing on the sand, or off collecting shells and seaweed. She wouldn't have been so cowed, so diffident. And I make a decision: I want my mermaid back. It's as if the cold water has brought me some clarity, some purpose. It's time to push a little –starting with my own confession.

"I'm sorry," I say when I reach her. "I'm sorry I failed you, Lucy."

She turns to me and I see confusion in her face.

"Is that what you think?"

I nod, not trusting myself to speak.

She stares off at the sea again. "And I'm sitting here thinking about how I've let you down. How ashamed Dad would have been."

I'm shocked. "Never, Lucy," I manage. "You must never feel ashamed."

"He's still controlling me, isn't he?" she says. "He's controlling both of us. I'm still not free of him."

She's suddenly on her feet, startling a nearby gull into the air. Its scolding cries fill the space around us.

"No," she says, quiet but determined. "There's no-one to blame but him. He's the only one who should feel any shame." Then she sheds her clothes and runs to the sea.

When she gets back to me she's shivering and I wrap her in a towel, rub her shoulders. She crawls into my arms, like she did when she was little and it's as if a dam has burst. Words pour out of her, unshaped, unmoulded – the unedited version. All I can do is listen. Then we sit in silence, oblivious to everyone else, everything else. When we get home we are exhausted - ozone and emotion have drained us both and we crave nothing but sleep.

***

I wake up to the smell of lemons. At first I think I'm still dreaming – of islands and blue seas and lemon trees. But then I realise that the smell is real, that I've just woven it into my dreams. I can hear the echoes of cooking, the clatter of pans and dishes. Then a thick, warm scent – eggs and butter and sugar. It seems to drift around me, wrap me up and beckon me downstairs.

Lucy is at the oven and she turns to me as I enter the kitchen. She's smiling. Not a full beam, high voltage smile like it used to be. Just a tiny smile, curving the corners of her mouth, but it reaches her eyes for the first time in weeks.

Just a tiny smile, but like oxygen to me all the same, a sudden gasp of air. I can see my little girl again in that smile.

She holds out a plate to me – drowning in lemon juice and sparkling with sugar. "Pancakes," she says.

Tracey Glasspool lives in Devon with her husband, three sons, sheep, llamas, cats and snake. She has been writing seriously for about three years now and during that time has had stories for adults and children published in magazines, short story collections and online.

She is addicted to entering competitions and has been lucky enough to win or be placed in several. As well as the thrill of winning Hysteria 2014, she has also won first place in the Choc Lit winter competition 2013, Exeter Writers Short Story Comp 2013/14, plus a win with Writers Forum magazine and a second place in Writing Magazine, amongst others.

She recently joined Exeter Writers and is a member of an online critique group.

She works part-time as an administrator in a small, rural primary school and is working, very slowly, on her first novel.

The Gift – Marcia Woolf

Nuala O'Donnell had a crystal ball, which she kept on her desk at work. It started out, like so many things in the office, as a joke. One Christmas it was presented to her, beautifully boxed and wrapped and tied with a silver bow. A small tag indicated it was for her, but the name had been typed onto a label and stuck on, and there was no clue as to its origin other than that someone had, under the anonymity of the "secret Santa" cloak, made fun at her expense.

Nuala's boss, Derek, thought it was hilarious. He proposed leaving his mobile phone switched off even more than usual on the basis that she merely had to consult her crystal to know where he was, what he was doing and why he was late for his next meeting. Likewise, he could henceforth and with impunity submit to her undated expense claims, half-written letters, obscure messages on post-it notes and incomplete telephone numbers and, as if by magic, Nuala would be able to make good his deficiency. She would know and see all, like the Great Panjandrum, the Oracle, the Font of all Wisdom! Wasn't second sight a gift of the faeries and the leprechauns after all?

Once the joking and the Christmas party were over, Nuala was even less pleased with her gift. It was too heavy for her to ever want to put it in her bag and take it home, so it stayed in the office gathering a film of dust. Occasionally she gave it a wipe with a tissue. Not wishing to cause offence to the mystery benefactor, she was reluctant to throw it away, although the temptation was sometimes strong, not least the time it toppled unaccountably from its little metal stand, rolled across the desk and landed on her foot. She had a bruise for weeks. It was, thought Nuala, possibly the most useless, unattractive and insulting thing she had ever received. Had it worked, of course, it would have been the most highly-valued piece of equipment in the room, but it didn't. Not a glimmer or hint of foreknowledge or prognostication did it ever emit: an upturned goldfish bowl would have offered as much insight.

Unfortunately for Nuala, her boss, an insensitive man at the best of times, continued to be delighted by the prospect of an all-seeing assistant, and from time to time would use this flimsy excuse to play practical jokes on her. Once he leapt out at her from behind the stationery cupboard. "Aha!" he cried, waving his arms around, "you didn't see that in your crystal ball!" as Nuala gasped for breath and tried not to drop her box of envelopes.

The problem with the crystal ball was that, far from aiding in the daily tasks, it made things worse because Nuala spent so much time deciphering cryptic notes and playing detective. Her job became increasingly testing, and each day it seemed she had to stay a little longer to complete the work in hand. One Friday, when everyone else had gone home or to the pub, Nuala found herself sitting at her desk to the quiet tick of the clock, attempting to tally an apparently random set of VAT calculations, when something moved, just on the edge of her peripheral vision, next to the telephone. For a second or two she froze: her first thought was that it was a mouse, but then she refocused and, to her surprise, she realised that there was an image floating inside the crystal ball. Nuala put down her pen and looked around the office. It was empty: no-one could be playing an elaborate trick on her, surely?

***

The image, initially small, cloudy and inverted, began to clear and grow. It now filled the ball to its surface, although still upside down and distorted by the curve of the glass. She reached out and delicately tried to turn the ball on its stand, but the scene remained static and the wrong way round. She tilted her head sideways: the ball was showing her the sitting room of an ordinary domestic house. It really was very odd. As she continued to watch, the picture trembled as if it were expanding inside the ball but could not break its boundary. Suddenly the scene in the sphere shuddered violently and appeared to pop: Nuala raised her hands to her face, half-expecting the glass to shatter, but when she dared peep at it again she was amazed to see that the image had now righted itself and there, plainly visible in the fish-eye lens, was the same sitting room. A moment later, two figures appeared. One she recognised immediately as her boss, and Nuala gave a little "oh!" of surprise. She glanced around again. There really was not a soul apart from her in the room. How on earth could she explain this with no-one to vouch for her? Anyone would think she had gone mad! Peering closer into the ball, Nuala guessed that the other figure must be Derek's wife, and that this was their home. It was most unnerving, like spying with a hidden camera. She wondered if they were aware of her presence, although that was unlikely as they were moving around and seemingly talking quite normally. Nuala tapped the desk in frustration. If only she could hear what they were saying.

Gently she moved the ball left and right, and learnt that she could see more of the interior: by turning it through 180 degrees she had a view of the other side of the room. Then she spotted something very weird indeed: why did Derek have a Christmas tree in his house in July? This just confirmed what she had long suspected; that he was a complete nutter. Actually, after a few minutes, and once the immediate novelty had waned, Nuala found the domestic goings-on remarkably dull. It was like watching a very bad TV soap with the sound off. She checked her watch: nearly seven thirty. What a crazy waste of time! Nuala decided to put the ball into her desk drawer and go home. There was no off-switch, obviously, so she hoped it might go into sleep mode or something once it was in darkness.

She began to tidy her things away. Nuala hated leaving stuff lying around. Her colleagues sometimes thought that she had gone away on holiday when in fact she had only popped out to the loo. Still, there were worse habits than tidiness and, being conscientious but also something of a pessimist, it had occurred to her that, should she have the misfortune to meet an untimely death between the end of one working day and the start of the next, then at least no-one would have an awful mess to sort out.

Clearing done, Nuala was just about to pick up the crystal when she noticed something else: her boss's wife was wrapping Christmas presents. And, sure enough, clear as could be, there was the very same box tied with the very same ribbon that had been given to her seven months previously. Adding insult to injury, she watched as Derek's wife showed him the typewritten label, and saw him laughing at it. Silently, of course. Nuala was furious. What a fool she'd been, sitting here late on a Friday when he was off home for the weekend! How he must have been congratulating himself, the smug, lazy, good-for-nothing that he was.

***

Nuala snatched up the ball, marched into her boss's office and dumped it right in the middle of his desk. Then she took an envelope, wrote his name in large angry capitals on the front and propped it against the vile object. She put on her jacket, took a final look around, and turned off the lights. She had briefly considered putting her resignation letter in the envelope, but writing it would have made her miss her train. Anyway, it didn't matter: now he had the crystal ball he'd know what it would have said. And, thought Nuala with satisfaction as she locked the door behind her, he certainly won't have seen that coming.

Marcia Woolf. I live in East Sussex, on the South Coast. I've written since I was very young but have only recently begun to think about becoming a published author. I joined a local Writers Group a couple of years ago, which gave me the push I needed to enter competitions. This is my first published work, one of around 17 short stories that I have put together under the collective working title Damage. Some of these (Battersea, Human Resources, Face Value) have been long-listed in other competitions this year. Many of the stories are darkly humorous, and I like to contrast the weird with the everyday; disturbing and unexpected events interrupting the flow of ordinary life. My first novel, Roadkill, is nearing completion.

Website: marciawoolf.com

Green Tea and Chocolate Fudge Cake – Olga Wojtas

Charlotte looked doubtfully at the Valentine card. It was too pink and pretty for her taste.

"It's lovely," she said. "So who's it for?"

"Steve," said Anna.

"Steve," repeated Charlotte, in a bright, conversational tone.

Anna reached across the cafe table and snatched the card back.

"You see, this is exactly why I don't tell you things," she snapped. "You are so judgmental."

Charlotte said nothing.

"Oh, go ahead and say it," Anna went on. "You always thought he was a bastard. But I've been thinking about it, and I just over-reacted. You know what Fiona Reid's like. She led him on. And they were only snogging."

She reached down for her handbag and took out her pen.

"But don't worry. I was going to ask you to help me, but I can see that would make you uncomfortable."

She signalled to the waiter. "Hi, I'd like an organic green tea and some carrot cake. And I'm sending this Valentine to my boyfriend, well, my ex-boyfriend, really, and I don't want him to recognize the writing. Could you put 'I miss you – let's try again'?"

The waiter did as he was told.

"Thanks. And could you draw a heart underneath with an arrow through it?"

The waiter glanced at Charlotte.

"Just a latte for me, and a piece of millionaire's shortbread, please," said Charlotte.

***

"I'll have chocolate fudge cake with cream, and a hot chocolate. With cream in that too, and marshmallows," Anna told the waiter.

Charlotte grimaced in sympathy at the calorie-laden order. "So he still hasn't got in touch?"

"Much worse than that. Much, much worse than that."

Charlotte waited until the cake arrived and Anna could fortify herself with the frosted icing.

"Worse than him not getting in touch?" she prompted.

Anna laid down the fork. "I got in touch with him. Oh, enough with that look, already! It seemed a good idea at the time. I thought the Valentine might have got lost in the post. I bumped into him outside his office. Okay, yes, so maybe I waited for him outside his office. He'd got the card all right. He just hadn't realized it was from me."

She scooped a reckless amount of cake into her mouth as she continued.

"Sorry?" said Charlotte.

Anna swallowed with difficulty.

"I said, he thought it was from Lizzie Rivers."

Charlotte's eyes widened in shock.

"I know," said Anna. "The shoes she wears!"

Charlotte took a gulp of latte to help her recover. "Now, why would he think a message saying 'I miss you – let's try again' was from Lizzie Rivers?"

Anna slumped. "Yeah, yeah. Because he'd been going out with her. And since you ask, he'd been going out with her for much of the time he was going out with me."

Charlotte stroked her arm sympathetically.

"The bastard," she said. "May he die horribly and rot in hell."

She broke the millionaire's shortbread into two and passed the larger piece to Anna.

"Thanks," said Anna.

"You're welcome," said Charlotte.

"I don't mean the millionaire's shortbread," said Anna.

"I know," said Charlotte.

***

"Organic green tea, please. Nothing to eat," Anna told the waiter.

Charlotte's eyes narrowed. "What's going on?"

Anna took a deep breath. "I'm getting married. What? Don't look at me like that! You're the first person I've told. I couldn't have told you any earlier, we only decided yesterday."

"We?"

"Steve and me."

"Steve?"

"God, it's like a police interrogation! I knew you'd be like this, that's why I didn't say anything before. Okay, I've been seeing him for a while, a few weeks maybe. He rang me, well, maybe I rang him, and it turned out things weren't going well between him and Lizzie and we – we got back together. Look, I'm getting married! You're supposed to be happy for me!"

"Tell me you're joking."

"And I want you to be my bridesmaid. I've been thinking about your dress all day, full length lilac silk, and purple flowers in your hair. You will look so hot, nobody will even bother looking at me."

"Just tell me you're joking."

"I think St Dominic's is nice, and Auntie Emily knows the vicar, I'm sure she can talk him round even though we don't go there. Steve says - "

"Steve is a bastard."

"That's my fiancé you're talking about."

"Have you forgotten? Have you forgotten finding him with his tongue down Fiona Reid's throat – in the middle of your birthday party? And he was doing a lot more than that with Lizzie Rivers."

"They're slags. He's a red-blooded male. He's not going to turn it down if it's offered to him on a plate."

"Am I a slag?"

"What?"

"Am – I – a – slag?"

"What?"

"Okay, sometimes you don't tell me things, sometimes I don't tell you things either. At your birthday party – he was hitting on me."

"That's just his way. He's very flirtatious. He doesn't mean anything by it."

"Excuse me. He was not being flirtatious. He was trying to cop a feel. I told him I was a black belt in Tae Kwon Do and I would break all his fingers. He said he loved it when I talked dirty. He's a bastard."

"You're making this up," said Anna. Why haven't you told me this before?"

"Because you caught him with Fiona Reid, and you dumped him, and you were upset enough."

"He's changed. We had a big talk and he says he's ready for commitment. I want you to be my bridesmaid."

"Don't," said Charlotte.

Anna caught hold of her hand. "You're my best friend," she said.

Charlotte stared down at the table. "He's a bastard."

***

Charlotte couldn't bear to have one more person ask her what her bridesmaid's dress looked like. She slipped out of the hotel ballroom's side door into an empty corridor and leaned her forehead against the coolness of the wall. Then she felt a particularly unpleasant sensation.

"Hey there," said Steve.

Charlotte wished she really was a black belt in Tae Kwon Do. She would break all his fingers, then rip his arm off and stuff it down his throat. Groping the future bridesmaid during his engagement party suggested that his level of commitment to his fiancée was not as high as Anna thought.

And in that moment, Charlotte hatched her plan.

"Hey," she said in a breathy Marilyn Monroe voice, quite unlike her own, "easy, tiger!"

"Mm," said Steve, looming over her, "you're a bit more friendly than usual."

"It must be the attraction of forbidden fruit. You've always been so – available before, and here you are, practically a married man."

Stop talking such total garbage, she thought. He's never going to fall for it. Then she yelped. He had fallen for it.

"No, not now!" she said urgently. "Anna's mum and dad are just leaving, and I've got to say goodbye to them. Tell you what – in there, the ladies' – I'll meet you in five minutes. Okay?"

She fled back into the ballroom and downed the nearest glass of Champagne. Then she went in search of Anna.

"We have to talk. Privately."

Anna's expression turned stubborn. "I'm marrying him. And nothing you can say is going to change that."

"I know," said Charlotte. "I know. But this is really, really important. Meet me in the loo in four minutes – no, three minutes. And do not be late."

Steve pulled Charlotte into the furthest cubicle. It was very cramped.

"Okay," he murmured encouragingly. "If you shift a bit to the left and put your right foot there - "

"You've done this before, haven't you?" said Charlotte.

He gave a seductive chuckle. "Jealous?"

Charlotte quickly reverted to Marilyn Monroe mode. "No, it's very exciting to be with someone so – experienced."

There was the sound of a zip being unfastened.

"Now if you just - " breathed Steve.

"I can't!" said Charlotte in a panic. "My skirt's too tight. I'm going to fall. I've got no sense of balance."

"Lean against the wall," said Steve, a trifle irritably.

"No, that's no good – the toilet-roll's in the way. This isn't going to work."

Four things then happened in quick succession.

First, Steve tugged impatiently at Charlotte's skirt, ripping the seam.

Second, Anna came into the ladies' and said: "Charlotte? Are you in here?"

Third, Charlotte pulled open the cubicle lock, and she and Steve toppled out in an indecently dishevelled heap.

Fourth, a group of women burst in, flourishing bottles of Champagne, and demanding to toast the bride-to-be.

Anna looked at Charlotte with a mixture of horror, dismay and rage.

"How could you?" she whispered.

Then she pushed her way through the throng of now-silent revellers, and left.

***

The large piece of apple pie lay untouched. Charlotte pretended to read the magazine she had brought with her, wondering how long she should wait before giving up and leaving.

There was a sudden scraping of metal on wood as Anna pulled out the chair opposite her and sat down.

Charlotte gave her a nervous smile. "I didn't know whether you'd turn up."

"You stupid mare," said Anna.

"God, Anna, I wasn't doing anything with him, you have to believe me! I was just trying to prove to you that you can't trust him."

"How daft do you think I am?" demanded Anna. "Of course I can't bloody trust him. That's the whole point."

Charlotte shifted in her seat. "Sorry?" she asked cautiously.

Anna leaned forward and helped herself to some apple pie.

"That was my plan from the start," she said, a little indistinctly. "Hey, good pie. Yes, my plan. The bastard. Two-timing me with that slag Lizzie Rivers. So I thought marry him, wait until he chases after the next one, find a good divorce lawyer, throw him out on the street. I get at least half the flat and with luck, some of his pension. Will you stop looking at me like that! This is exactly why I don't tell you things!"

"I don't believe this," said Charlotte. "I do not believe this. You decided to marry him just to get even?"

Anna shrugged. "You know of a better way? And now you've ruined all my plans. It would have been okay if I'd been the only one to see you, but there were just too many damn witnesses. They must be having a field day. My fiancé and my best friend – it's such a bloody cliché."

She sighed and took some more pie.

"He is a bastard," said Charlotte, still mourning the ripped skirt. "He deserves to suffer. I'm almost sorry the wedding's off."

The forkful of pie halted in mid-air as Anna stared at her in astonishment.

"Of course the wedding's not off," she said. "But I'm really sorry, Charlotte – with all of them seeing you like that, there's just no way you can be my bridesmaid."

Olga Wojtas is half-Polish and half-Scottish. She was born and brought up in Edinburgh where she now works as a writer and journalist. She attended the school which inspired Muriel Spark's "The Prime of Miss Jean Brodie".

She has taught in a French lycée, road-tested the Mazda RX-7, and is quite good at making soup. She began her journalistic career on the Evening Express in Aberdeen, and was Scottish editor of the Times Higher Education before going freelance in 2009. This has let her spend more time on creative writing, and she is the proud owner of a diploma in literature and creative writing from the Open University.

She has had a number of short stories published in literary magazines and anthologies in the UK and US, including Alliterati, The Mayo Review, New Writing Scotland and Luna Station Quarterly.

The Bridge – Katie Martin

You chose the blue patina. Dark, velvety Egyptian blue was your mother's favourite colour. It was hand-cast, solid brass. Robust but sensual too. 'A little like Catherine, then,' John said. He never had that filter every parent should have; the one that tells you what not to say to a child.

When they handed you the catalogue your index finger moved straight to the blue patina.

'That one,' you said, without a waver.

But the perfect blue looked less blue now. Blazed upon by a sulphurous high-season sun it was more purple than blue and you were frustrated that what had been perfect didn't feel perfect anymore. You told yourself the light was lying.

You weren't irritable because you were in Portofino – you'd wanted to come. But what you hadn't wanted, with an intensity of not wanting that was new to you, was for other people to join you. Family only was how you'd imagined it. You and your father, your memories undiluted by those of couples, like Anna and Peter, who had merely stepped into your mother's life   a dinner party here, a theatre trip there   and stepped out of it again.

You're never alone with a good book. Your mother used to tell you that. One of many of her sayings that replay themselves to you, waking, sleeping or in that restive ragged-edged state between the two. Odd how her words stay crisp when her face loses sharpness by the day. It's what memories do. You mustn't torture yourself with that.

Once she was gone you hid yourself away. And you read and you read until you began to suspect your mother had only been half-right; you're never alone with a good book, but you can still be lonely.

What you must try to remember is this: if she could mend your loneliness, your mother would do it. She would lend you her bow to slay Smaug, sponsor you in the Arena, be the Pan to your Lyra.

***

Your father hired the boat for two hours.

He eased it in until it abutted the jetty and reached out his arm to Anna. 'Ladies first'. Such a gentleman.

Anna's perfume was cloying in the salt air, as unpleasant here as you'd found it at the crematorium. An imposition of freesia and musk rose.

'Are we all going to fit?' Anna was struggling with her skimpy skirt. She clasped two handfuls of its muslin as she stretched out an evenly tanned leg towards the boat. Her fingernails and toenails were geranium red.

The day they burned your mother, Anna's fingernails were pink. Lurid. And you watched, fiercely mute, as the bubblegum took hold of your father's charcoal shoulder and squeezed.

'I'm always here for you,' you heard her whisper to him. You disliked the 'I'm'.

'This boat's designed for eight,' Peter reassured his wife. He was all patience. Too much patience can be worse than too little. 'No need to worry.'

You and Peter still stood side by side on the boardwalk. The same height already, and you only fourteen.

'Sit down! It might capsize!' Anna squealed and gave a decency tug at the hem of a skirt that hadn't the fabric to oblige. John half-sat, half-fell into the place beside her.

John was laughing, Anna was laughing, and Peter, all patience (his downfall, his life-sentence), stepped in next. Further up the walkway bored families in an excursion queue eyed you enviously. Bobbing around for a couple of hours, taking in the pastel collage of harbour-front hotels. What could be nicer? Perhaps they'd do that tomorrow.

You were still hesitant on the boardwalk. You clutched the purple patina tight into your chest feeling it shift inwards and outwards with your breaths.

'May I hold her for you?' Peter raised his arms to you in understanding.

You appreciated his pronoun so you let him take the urn, watching as he wrapped broad hands around it. You stepped down, the boat rocked and settled lower in the water.

'Thank you for trusting me with her,' Peter said.

'Don't overdo it,' you mumbled as you took back the urn.

The boat-owner unwound the ropes from the moorings and gave you a little push. Peter took the oars and you were off.

***

John sat closer to Anna than the boat's configuration required and you hated that. You concentrated hard on the seagull-snow coating the red roofs of the harbour-front hotels and cafés.

'We sailed along this stretch of coast before,' Anna said, 'before you were born, Gavin. Do you remember, John?'

'I remember you were sick as a parrot,' John said.

'Oh, you.' Anna laughed and ran her tongue across the surface of her gluey-gloss lips.

You remembered your mother's words then, as crisp as if she was here and speaking them: 'She'll probably live forever. No brain, no heart, nothing to go wrong.' Not your mother at her most charitable, but we all have our bad days.

And this had all the makings of a bad day for you. Anna shouldn't have been at your mother's funeral and she shouldn't be here. Anna was everywhere she shouldn't be.

'Do you need some Limoncello?' John asked her. She broke into ripples of laughter.

'Was my mother sick?' you asked, ignoring their private joke.

'No, she wasn't sick,' John said, continuing it.

'Catherine wasn't a sick kind of person,' Peter said.

'She was a lovely person.' Anna pulled a tissue from her handbag. She wasn't crying, so she twisted it between scarlet-tipped fingers instead. Her gluey lip wobbled.

'She was a lovely person,' John said.

'She was,' Peter said.

'No, she wasn't,' you said.

They all stared at you then. And Anna stopped twisting her tissue and forgot she'd been trying to cry.

'She wasn't "lovely",' you insisted, spurred on by their stares. 'She was spiteful and real and funny and cruel and I loved her.'

'We all loved her,' Anna said.

'We did,' John said.

'We did,' Peter said.

Anna reached across to lay her hand over yours.

'We all loved your mum, honey, but she was your mum. There's nobody in the world like a mum. Especially for a boy.'

'Like you'd know,' you said.

Your mother shouldn't have let you overhear that conversation. The one where she predicted Anna's infertility would be the death-knell for her marriage.

'What on earth do you mean?' John said. 'Anna's always said she doesn't want children.'

'She'll want them now,' your mother said, too loudly. Careless.

You'd inflicted your wound. Anna lifted the tissue to her eyes.

'That was uncalled for, Gavin,' John said.

Anna looked at Peter as if expecting words of comfort from him too. But Peter was silent. 'So?' she asked, hard done by. 'Who's going to do it?'

And if Peter didn't hear it was because he wasn't in Portofino now, but in Portofino then. Portofino before you came screaming and laughing and sulking into your mother's life making everything breathe.

John holds Anna's curls out of her face as she leans over the edge of the yacht. Settled on the deck's upholstered seats Peter and Catherine drink Limoncello from the bottle. When she's finished throwing up, Anna comes over to them. She wants Limoncello to settle her stomach, but between them Peter and Catherine have drained the lot. Anna brings her foot down hard onto the deck.

She's been sick. None of the rest of them has been sick.

'You are so selfish,' she tells them.

John says they'll dock at the next town and buy another bottle. Peter feels the lemon-scented warmth of Catherine's breath as she leans in to him and whispers, 'My husband   such a gentleman!'

And suddenly he is impatient. To see the lights of the next town appear around the cliff face. To dock. For John and Anna to start their search for Limoncello.

In time they dock and Peter and Catherine watch as her husband and his wife walk away from them, Anna tripping as they start across the lichen-frosted stone bridge. John righting her.

And when they are out of sight Peter and Catherine are silent for a few moments, watching the stars. Or pretending to.

When Catherine speaks, her voice is singsong over the lazy lap of the waves. 'We could sail away,' she says. 'They'd come back and we'd be gone.' Peter can see the moon's reflection in her eyes. The harbour lights cast shadows across her face making it look gaunt and hollow, almost ugly. He's never loved it more.

She closes her eyes then, drawing black-fringed shutters across the moon. 'Let's do it,' she says. 'Let's sail and sail in a straight line until we hit Africa. We can set up a school. I love children. You love children.'

She's drunk. She's ugly. She's beautiful. She has always been hopeless at geography. They couldn't sail in a straight line to Africa   Sardinia was in the way.

John and Anna's Limoncello-hunt lasted about an hour. A one-hour slice out of a single day out of all the days Peter and your mother had and would ever have. An hour's interlude in doing as they usually did and then back to that other life, that wrong life, as if that one hour had been all imagining.

***

'Who's going to do it?' Anna said again.

You clambered onto your knees, unable to countenance the idea that it should be anyone but you. The sun caught the gold enamelling and patterns of light skipped across the surface of the water.

Your mother caught you in the lungs. You breathed her in and rolled, coughing, on the bottom of the boat.

Your mother coated Anna's glue lips. She might have been kissing floured loaves.

Your mother got John in the eyes. He rubbed bunched fists into his sockets.

Your mother aged Peter. His black hair was more salt than pepper.

Your coughs became laughs.

'This isn't funny,' Anna said. Her tongue flicked across her lips – a reflex. And then she shuddered – another reflex.

'It most certainly is not,' John agreed.

'Mum,' you said, 'is laughing her arse off!'

**

You were right, of course. I laughed.

The four of you made such a peculiar picture on the crowded boardwalk. John's face was set to serious but there were flecks of me in his eyebrows yet. Tears (for in the end they had fallen) had bled flesh-coloured rivulets through Anna's powder mask. The two of them marched purposefully towards the hotel.

'You shouldn't have come,' you said to Peter. You and he hung back in their wake, keen to avoid catching them up. 'I wish you hadn't.' You didn't understand. Not yet.

'What do you mean?'

'It should have just been Dad and me.'

You'd found a solitary stone and begun to kick it up the boardwalk. You wanted to kick it all the way back. Up the street, over the bridge and all the way to your hotel like we used to at home in England, until, annoyed with my hopeless aim you'd take charge of the kicking. You'd ruckle your forehead in concentration and the tip of your tongue would stick out at the corner of your mouth. When did you stop doing that?

'I'm sorry.'

'Don't you mind?' You indicated Anna, now pretending to dust me from John's shirt-sleeve as if I were a cobweb. You minded very much and you wanted Peter to mind too.

But Peter didn't mind. 'Your mother and I. We were special. Here. A long time ago.'

You narrowed your eyes and the next kick you drove at that stone was as clumsy and off-aim as mine used to be.

'Stupid,' you said. But when you caught up with it again you landed it one precise final contact. You watched as it arced through the air and between a narrow gap in the lichened pillars that ran along the length of the bridge and as it dropped into the dark, velvety Egyptian blue beneath.

Katie Martin. When she's not being a mother in Cambridge or a lawyer in London, Katie writes and reads, reads and writes. She's finished one novel, is close to finishing her second (mostly written on commuter trains in size 6 font to avoid fellow passengers sneaking a peek) and has four more in their embryonic stages. She's also a keen writer of short stories, (arguably) overuses parentheses and drinks too much coffee.

In the spare time she doesn't have she's studying for an MA in Creative Writing (because writing, like other skills, *can* be honed and improved whatever the latest miseryguts bestselling writer alleges). She is also an active member of a Cambridge-based writers' group – the Penny University Writers' Club, which meets regularly to read and critique members' latest work, be it short stories, novels or poetry.
Website: puwriters.net and Twitter @K_A_Martin

Frustration – Margaret Skinner

It was the mug that did it.

Or rather the huge spider which she'd caught sight of at the back of the cupboard.

Unable to kill anything with a heart, she'd had to remove all the mugs on the shelf to get to it and Brian's one had been right at the back - somehow missed in the process of gradually getting rid of things in the months after his death. Seeing it again had completely unravelled her.

It had a squashed up face and pug nose with the handle in the shape of a cauliflower ear and was bought years ago while on an anniversary holiday in Barcelona. She had accompanied it with a card which said 'saw this and thought of you ...' and although it was supposed to have been just a token to mark the day, the main present being the holiday itself, it had made him smile and he had used it regularly in the mornings until the shaking had forced him to swap it for some awful plastic contraption with a straw.

Everything came back to her as though it had just been sitting in the wings, waiting for an innocent catalyst to catch her unawares and make her realise she still had to be wary of every corner, every nook and cranny and never believe she could be free of the heartache which reduced to her to tears every time.

Rowan's barking snapped Ruth out of her reverie and made her realise the postman must be passing outside. She had been standing rooted to the spot, caught in the raw grief, once again astonished by the impact when she had expected it to at least have lessened in intensity by now.

A soft 'thunk' on the mat confirmed it had indeed been the postman who had been getting an earful of Rowan's protective warning and, drying her eyes on the teatowel she replaced all the mugs in the cupboard again - Brian's included - and decided a dog walk might just be the thing to distract.

She owed him a long walk today. Yesterday had been so wet and miserable it was all she could do to drag herself round the block for 20 minutes and she felt she'd cheated him somehow. What else did he have to look forward to these days with only her misery for company?

She had to remember she was not the only one who had lost her best friend.

She picked up the post from the mat and idly glanced at the white A4 envelope at the bottom of the pile, recognising her own particular typescript font on the label.

Her heart skipped a beat.

Was it wise to open this now and risk the morning degenerating even further or wait until she got back and prolong the agony?

Knowing she'd never last out another hour, she ripped open the envelope and read the first line of the letter clipped to the attached manuscript.

Ruth gazed at the words in shock.

A laugh escaped her but it was a strange sound with a touch of irony. Rowan looked up at her startled.

"Sorry boy" she stroked the old head knowing if they didn't get a move on there would be an accident.

Dropping the letter on the coffee table, Ruth quickly flung on her jacket and boots, grabbing the lead and frisbee on the way out and, feeling better than she had for months, she walked through to the field at the back of the house, intent on making Rowan's walk as much fun as possible.

Flinging the frisbee across the field for him, she laughed again as he went bounding after it like a mad thing and then jumped as another dog went whizzing past her legs, intent in joining in the play.

"Well that's a sound I haven't heard in a while" came a voice from behind her and she turned to see her neighbour, Chrissie, hove into view.

Ruth smiled. "I take it that was Millie who just passed me a minute ago?"

This time they both laughed as they watched the two dogs play fighting over the frisbee, frantically holding on to each side of it as though their lives depended on it.

"So what's all this gaiety about then?" Chrissie asked as she threw Millie's ball in her direction to distract her.

"Oh nothing" Ruth replied "I just feel I've turned a bit of a corner this morning."

"Yeah? Well that's good news" Chrissie touched her neighbour's arm. "You've had a rough year of it my friend."

The two woman walked together as the dogs ambled behind them, falling into conversation easily, laughing at the ironies of life, the way it had been ever since they had first met a couple of years ago. In that same field, Ruth that day a dripping mess, too tired to stop the tears, sick of putting a face on for the world, the stress of caring for Brian taking its toll as the Parkinsons gripped both of them in its ugly vice.

Chrissie had come across her and instantly enveloped her in a warm hug without preamble, knowing this rather than words was what she needed.

She had offered the hand of friendship that day and continued to offer it, never interfering, creating a bond between them that had grown stronger the more they saw each other and which Ruth knew without doubt had been a lifesaver.

This was the one person she would feel safe sharing her innermost secrets with but ......

As they walked back to their street, Ruth said

"Want to come in for a coffee?"

"If you don't mind muddy paws all over your kitchen floor that would be nice" answered Chrissie.

"I wouldn't worry about that - they'll match the ones we made yesterday which are still there."

Ruth unlocked the door and went through to the kitchen to pop the kettle on, while the dogs flopped exhausted at her feet, ready for a well-earned nap.

Suddenly she realised she'd left the source of all the excitement this morning lying on the coffee table in the sitting room and hurriedly went back through.

"I'll just shift this stuff and make a bit of room" she said picking up the post and dumping it on the kitchen workshop, careful to place the letter face down.

Chrissie didn't notice, mainly because she had her nose in the first of the Fifty Shades of Grey trilogy.

"I can't believe you bought this rubbish - you've gone right down in my estimation now" she said with a big grin on her face.

"Just wanted to see what all the fuss was about" Ruth replied not looking at her.

"Sure you did. Is it the slightest bit racy then?"

"It has its moments."

"Think I'd prefer the real thing to reading about it" Chrissie murmured.

Instantly her hand flew to her mouth.

"Oh Ruth I'm sorry - I didn't think!"

"Oh for heaven's sake Chris you don't have to walk on eggshells with me."

"I'm such an idiot though! It must be really hard."

"I wish!"

They both giggled and Ruth went through to sort out the tea.

"So how's the writing going?" Chrissie asked on her return. "Is it worse now that the course has finished?"

"Funnily enough no. Actually I'm really proud of myself Chrissie - I've managed to write for a couple of hours a day no matter how I'm feeling and often it's been much longer - it's almost pouring out of me."

"Pretty therapeutic then?"

"Without a doubt. Some days an absolute godsend truth be told."

"Are you doing anything with it though? Sending stuff off - that sort of thing?"

"Bits and pieces."

"Any joy?"

Ruth looked at her friend. She felt like she'd known this woman all her life rather than just two years and she knew for a fact she would be in a much worse place right now if it hadn't been for Chrissie this past year.

"Can you keep a secret?"

Chrissie looked at her quizzically.

Ruth got up and went through to the kitchen, picked up the letter and placed it on the table in front of her friend. As Chrissie picked it up and started reading it her eyes grew wide.

"Ruth that's brilliant - well done! Oh wow I can't believe you kept that to yourself for the past hour!"

"There's a reason for that Chris - look at the top of the letter."

Chrissie glanced up to the letterhead and almost fell off the chair.

"You dark horse!" she squealed.

"Just because Brian's gone it doesn't mean I've turned to stone you know." Ruth leaned over and took the letter from her friend, looking at her seriously.

"Please swear you won't tell anyone - on your life" she pleaded.

Chrissie made a zip motion across her mouth as she said "My lips are sealed."

Then she burst out laughing.

"Of course you'll have to let me read it - part of the deal."

"Noooooooooooooo!" squealed Ruth. "I'll never look you in the face again!"

"... except I saw the name of the magazine remember ..."

"You wouldn't!"

"Oh the agony in that face! Okay then I'll be a good friend. I'm telling your mum though."

Ruth pushed her playfully. "Don't you dare! Anyway she wouldn't know what it was about."

Chrissie got up and pulled her jacket off the peg as Millie trotted through at the sound of the front door opening.

"You have a point there. Erotica Monthly isn't exactly People's Friend is it?"

She turned to her friend, her heart lifted by the sight of this changed face before her – the one she had seen so much pain in during the past two years and the one she had longed to see joy in again.

"Word of advice girl. Keep scribbling. But next time get accepted somewhere you can actually tell folk about?"

Ruth hugged her.

"Jealousy's a terrible emotion" she laughed.

Margaret Skinner. I'm a 56 year old menopausal grandmother living in Aberdeen with 3 cats who boss me around on a regular basis. In love with the printed word from a young age, it was only after undertaking an Open University Creative Writing course in 2011 that I plucked up courage and submitted a story to 'People's Friend'. Happily they accepted it and have since taken another one plus five feature articles - I've also had three features published in 'Scottish Memories' and come second in a flash fiction competition. I'm delighted to be runner up in the Hysteria competition but as it's the second time – note to self - must try harder ......

I was recently diagnosed with dysthymia (a mild form of chronic depression) and took a break from work in June to try and find ways of getting better. I found journal writing a fantastic form of therapy but now tend to do too much of that and not enough of the creative stuff!

I don't have a website but if anyone wants to get in touch please feel free to e-mail me at margc@talk21.com

Dover Calais – Linda McVeigh

Rebecca looked down at the grey water. A broken plastic bucket floated on its oil-slicked surface, alongside discarded carrier bags and fragments of shattered timber. Filthy. People swim in that, she thought, like that man, the tall one, the comedian. Irritation rose in her. What was his name? The fog in her brain should have cleared by now – it had been almost four months, after all – but she still felt lost, unable to concentrate for more than a few seconds before intrusive thoughts overwhelmed her.

She'd been quietly determined when she left home that morning, but, as the cold seeped through her flimsy cardigan and into her bones, she began to have second thoughts. Maybe she should leave the deck and find a warm, quiet corner of the bar to sit in. She could have a glass of wine, forget the whole plan – just wait for the boat to dock in Calais, then turn around and go back home again. But she'd been feeling queasy since the ferry pulled out of Dover and didn't think she could stomach it.

The weight of her rucksack pulled at her shoulders, making her back ache, so she pulled it off and set it on the deck between her feet. She leaned further over the guard rail and studied the water again. What was wrong with people, littering the sea like that? She wondered whether it was the same on the sea bed, whether it was all piling up down there – a massive, underwater rubbish dump that would one day silt up the whole Channel.

Mark used to talk about the floating islands of rubbish he'd seen in the Pacific when he was a steward on cruise ships. He'd even shown her photographs, so she supposed it was true. He'd worn his uniform on their wedding day – white cotton and gold braiding – and her friends had teased her, saying it was like something out of An Officer and a Gentleman, that they never thought she'd go overboard for a sailor. Even her parents were swept away by his charm – their warnings about marrying in haste evaporating within hours of meeting him. Her mother called her a lucky girl, saying she could see why she hadn't wanted to let this one slip through the net, but Rebecca didn't feel so lucky when he went back to sea two weeks after their wedding, leaving her alone again.

He was gone almost twelve weeks that first time – long enough for her to start believing she'd imagined everything: the hasty courtship, the wedding, the brief honeymoon in Barcelona. She remembered coming in from work one day, just before his return, looking around the flat and realising there was hardly a trace of him – a couple of shirts in the wardrobe, a few CDs, an almost-empty can of shaving foam. He said he didn't believe in possessions, that the travelling life had shown him you didn't need all that stuff weighing you down. And all the time, there she was – alone in their rented flat – accumulating crockery and bed linen, wishing away the weeks and months, waiting for his return, so their time together could begin properly.

She got used to the long absences eventually, began to make light of them, telling her friends and herself that she had the best of both worlds – that the days they spent together when he was on leave were like a honeymoon, making the extended separations almost worthwhile. But when he returned from a cruise of the Eastern Mediterranean and made his big announcement she felt betrayed. Cruise ships were one thing, but the real navy? She always imagined he'd get a job on dry land eventually... settle down – not that he'd ever made her any such promise.

'But why?' she asked him. 'Don't you have to sign up for a minimum period or something?'

'It'll fly by, Becky. In the meantime, it's better money and better prospects. It'll give me a proper trade, something I can be proud of.'

She started crying when he said he was doing it for her, for their future together. She didn't mean to; it was just so unexpected.

'I won't go if it upsets you so much,' he said. 'There's a cooling-off period if you're really against it... We'll manage somehow, I suppose.'

But Rebecca didn't want to be that kind of woman: the type who'd hold a man back, anchor him down. A submarine, though... She hadn't expected that. 'But what will you be doing down there?' she asked, when she got her voice back. 'What do people actually do on submarines?'

'I can't really talk about it,' he said. 'It's classified. Hush-hush. Besides, I don't want you worrying; you know how you are.'

She worried anyway. It was something about the word 'nuclear' that made it impossible not to. He told her all submarines were nuclear-powered nowadays, but she wasn't reassured and every time he went away all she could think about was that heavy, grey capsule, right at the bottom of the sea with the crushing weight of tons and tons of water pushing down on it. When he came back to her, he told her about the claustrophobia, the stale smell of other men's bodies, the repetitive diet. 'I lie awake some nights,' he told her, 'dreaming about stupid, ordinary stuff, like sitting down to a nice dinner with you. I imagine us out in the fresh air together, walking in the woods, or sitting in the garden of a country pub somewhere...'

Not that he was often in the mood for talking about his underwater life. 'What's there to say, Becky, when every day is more or less the same?' Then he'd smother her questions with his lips, saying, 'God, I missed you. You've no idea.'

***

'Um... Excuse me.'

The young man who approached her was barely out of his teens, the skin on his neck covered with raw-looking pimples, his cheap bow tie slightly askew. He turned to look back at the doorway to the bar, where another young man waited with an encouraging look on his face.

'We was wondering...' he said. 'We was wondering if you was okay.'

'Yes... I...' She looked around her. The sky was a furious grey with dense clouds blackening the horizon. She was the only person still on deck. She pulled her cardigan around her. 'I'm fine, thank you.'

The boy looked at her doubtfully, while the other young man remained hunched in the doorway.

'Only it's gonna rain in a bit.' He spoke slowly and loudly, as if she was deaf or stupid.

She nodded vaguely. 'I suppose it is.'

Still he hovered.

It dawned on her what he and his friend might be thinking, how it must look, the way she was leaning over the guardrail. She pulled herself upright and took a step back. 'I felt a bit sick,' she explained. 'I'm better out here in the fresh air.'

The young man considered her for a few seconds before wandering back to his friend, apparently satisfied that she wasn't going to do anything silly.

***

They were married six years in all. No children. She supposed, in the circumstances, that it was just as well. She always thought she wanted them, but he'd persuaded her it wasn't fair, what with him being away so much. 'No hurry,' he used to say, 'we've got years ahead of us.' But she was thirty-six now and couldn't even imagine starting again with someone else, let alone trusting them enough to think about babies.

She'd been confused when the police turned up at the flat, felt all her worst fears flood over her. A fatal accident, they told her, once they'd come inside and made sure she was sitting down. She knew it. Something terrible had happened down there on the sea bed, a catastrophic failure of oxygen, an explosion... She'd almost collapsed into the policewoman's arms, unable to hear what was being said because of the shock thrumming in her ears, so it was a while before she understood what they were saying.

'A car crash?'

He must have been on his way to her, intending to surprise her with an unexpected shore leave. He wasn't much good at birthdays or anniversaries, but he must have remembered this one and decided to turn up unannounced –

'A van, actually,' the policewoman said.

'He was hit by a van?'

'No. There were no other vehicles involved. His van hit a concrete post on the M6. It looks like he fell asleep at the wheel.'

'A van? Why was he in a van? And isn't the M6 up north somewhere?'

She was aware of the officers exchanging a glance. 'Mrs Edwards,' the policewoman said, 'when was the last time you saw your husband?

***

How could she grieve for someone she didn't know? That's what was so impossible: the knowledge that her husband was a stranger. A lying stranger. She'd read about cases like this in the newspaper, wondered at the victims' gullibility, and now here she was. She hadn't told her friends or parents the truth; she'd had enough humiliation. That's why she hadn't let the other woman come to the funeral, despite the begging text messages. 'I only want to say goodbye,' the woman wrote. Imagine that. Imagine the other woman turning up at your husband's funeral. Try explaining that away.

She agreed to meet her briefly. The Police Family Liaison Officer suggested it, said it might help come to terms with things. The woman had two children with her and another on the way by the look of it. Rebecca didn't ask, didn't want to get sucked in. She tried to find it in her heart to sympathise with them, to see the situation from their point of view, but she couldn't. She had enough on her plate as it was.

***

Through the mist and rain, Rebecca could just about make out France. They'd be docking soon – she probably only had ten minutes or so. She was aware that one of the young men was still loitering by the bar door, pretending not to watch her. She picked up her rucksack and moved towards the guardrail. She undid the buckle, loosened the drawstring and pulled out the box. Once again, she was surprised by its weight – it was only ash, after all. The crematorium had offered her a choice of container, but she'd opted for the standard plain cardboard rectangle, not unlike a sturdy shoe box. She supposed she should say something, even if it was just in her head, but what words would suit an occasion like this?

She'd sealed the box that morning, using yards of gaffer tape, working quite neatly at first, but giving up when her shaking hands got the better of her. As she threw the box overboard, the young man lurched forward, then stopped and walked back to the shelter of the doorway, hands in pockets. For a moment she thought the box might float, but the hole she'd made in the top, roughly where a periscope might go, did what she hoped it would, letting the seawater flood in and pushing it beneath the grey, unforgiving waves.

Linda McVeigh has won several UK short-story competitions, including first prize in the Charleston Small Wonder Short Story Festival slam (in 2007 and again in 2011), first prize in the Rainy Cities Short Stories prize in 2010, and first prize in the 2011 Asham Award, judged by Sarah Waters. She also took first in the inaugural Brighton Prize, judged by Bethan Roberts and Laura Lockington. Her story 'All Over the Place' was published in 'Something Was There' (Virago, 2011). She is currently wrestling with a novel.

Discipline – Alison Wassell

On the first morning the headmaster hauled a boy out to the front and sent another scurrying to fetch the slipper. The slipper turned out to be an old plimsoll. The children called these things galoshes. Where Ruth came from, galoshes were what you wore in the rain. The language barrier lay between them, from the beginning.

The offending boy was in Ruth's class. His crime was unclear, but the punishment was obviously familiar. John Green bent over, clutching his grubby knees. Ruth flinched as the rubber sole struck the child's buttock. John Green did not. When it was over he straightened himself and returned to his place, exchanging a half smile with the boy next to him. The headmaster continued his lecture, hitting the palm of his hand with the plimsoll as he spoke.

Ruth's squeamishness had not gone unnoticed. As she led her class out of the hall the headmaster placed a fatherly hand on her arm.

'It's the only language they understand,' he whispered. Ruth nodded, silently vowing that she would never strike a child.

Perching on her desk, she smiled brightly

'I just know I am going to love teaching you,' she told her class. The children stared blankly back at her, with apparently no expectation of anyone loving anything to do with them. Several of them vigorously scratched their heads, until Ruth felt her own scalp begin to itch. She chose a girl on the front row.

'Would you like to give these books out for me?' she asked. The child shook her head. Ruth's smile froze. The girl sucked the end of her pigtail. Ruth dumped the pile of books on her desk.

'Give them out,' she demanded her voice girlishly high-pitched. The child shambled down the aisles between the desks, tossing the books

86

carelessly to the left and right. Some of them fell to the floor. Afraid to make an enemy of this surly child, Ruth swallowed a reprimand.

In the beginning Ruth was full of hope. Her college tutor had described children as sponges, ready to soak up knowledge. The analogy had seemed a good one. But these children were maddeningly incurious. The questions she asked hit their hard shells and bounced back unanswered. She was loath to admit that her new pupils repulsed her. They were grubby, and the dirt was not superficial, but ingrained. They smelled, with clothes that were changed only rarely and stained, grey underwear. When they undressed for physical education she could hardly bear to look at them.

Even their speech disgusted her.

'Can I go to't bog?' they asked. She tried to train them.

'Please may I be excused?' she instructed them to say. They gazed at her, not understanding.

'I need t'bog,' they said, clutching at themselves. She shooed them hurriedly out of the classroom.

Other classes marched into assembly in orderly lines. Only Ruth's pupils barged and chattered, pushed and straggled. The other teachers peered disapprovingly over their glasses. They all seemed to wear glasses, purely for this purpose.

In the classroom, the children lounged and sprawled, tipping back on their chairs and talking as she attempted to instruct them.

'A chair has four legs. If you only need two, you should stand up,' she said. Her wit was wasted on them.

The headmaster 'popped in' to see how she was getting on. His visit, inevitably, coincided with one of the children's most unruly episodes, as they composed a symphony of banging desk lids while she stood helpless at the blackboard, chalk in hand. He silenced them with a single look, clicking the classroom door shut. As one, they rose to their feet, hands clasped behind their backs as they chorused a greeting.

'Good morning, Mr Nash.' Ruth felt her cheeks grow warm as the headmaster asked if the class had been behaving. He raised his eyebrows when she assured him that they had. With a curt nod he gave them permission to sit down. They sat with none of the chair scraping that set her teeth on edge whenever they took their seats for her. Swivelling on his heels, he left the room. He could hardly have reached his office before the desk lid banging resumed.

When the last child had straggled home Mr Nash returned. Ruth rose, struggling not to chant a welcome. His manner was paternal. She did her best to convince him that things were going well. She had to admit that the children had taken a little getting used to. She laughed nervously.

In her interview she had mentioned that she was to be married the following summer. How did her intended feel, Mr Nash asked now, about her continuing to teach after the wedding? He might perhaps prefer her to stay at home and keep house for him. Ruth bristled. She had no plans to give up teaching. Mr Nash smiled indulgently. No doubt there would be a little one on the way before too long. His own wife had found her hands full with raising a family.

Fuelled by anger, Ruth grew determined. She recalled the words of her tutor,

'Find something they are interested in, and build on that.' She found it hard to imagine her class being interested in anything. She thought of John Green, the slippered boy, who was the grubbiest, and the dullest of them all, but the one they all followed. . She read the notes his previous teacher had written about him.

'Very backward. Does not wish to be anything else.' Ruth felt her anger surge again, this time on John Green's behalf. She would be the one to save him.

***

On Monday morning she summoned the boy to her desk with his reading book. He tossed the dog-eared text down and stood, head down, his hands in the pockets of his shorts. He had been on the same book since the beginning of term; a book intended for infants, full of simple sentences describing the contented life of Dick and Dora. John Green placed his grubby finger under the words as he read. Ruth turned aside slightly, shielding her mouth and nose from the smell of him.

The child read as though words were his enemies. He fought with even the simplest of them, with no attempt to make sense of what he read. When his finger made contact with a letter he recognised he barked out whatever word he could think of that began with that sound. Even his knowledge of the alphabet was insecure. After only one page he conceded defeat, clenching his hand into a fist and banging it on the desk. Beneath the grime, his cheeks flushed pink. Ruth closed the book and set it aside.

'What a boring story this is,' she said. John Green eyed her suspiciously. Reading was so much easier when it was about something you were interested in. Ruth rested her chin thoughtfully on her hands as she smiled at John Green. She wondered what he was interested in. John Green shrugged and looked down at his fist.

'Dunno,' he mumbled. Ruth was in no mood to be discouraged. She reeled off a string of potential boyish passions. John Green shook his head at each one. His eyes wandered to the window. In the playground a dog chased a pigeon.

'How about trains?' asked Ruth. She was nearing the end of her mental list. John Green's attention snapped suddenly back from the kerfuffle in the yard. His eyes met Ruth's for the first time that day. He nodded eagerly. His dad was a train driver, he said.

An eavesdropper on the front row snorted. It was well known that John Green's father was a habitual petty criminal, 'in and out of prison like a boomerang,' as another member of staff had informed Ruth. Ruth glared at the snorting child, then clapped her hands in excitement. That was it, she promised him. She would find him a book about trains.

Her promise was a rash one. She searched the sparsely populated shelves of the school library, then the public library, and finally the boxes in her parents' attic to which her brother's childhood reading matter had been consigned. There was, it seemed, no book on trains for a reader of John Green's level of ability.

'Have you found one?' he asked. Ruth shook her head. He smirked, as though pleased to have his lack of faith in her confirmed.

***

She purchased a child's scrapbook and, at home, set to work with scissors and glue, hacking at her brother's old annuals and magazines. Beneath each picture, in clear bold print, she wrote a caption, containing only the simplest vocabulary. She smiled to herself, satisfied that she had not let John Green down.

Proudly, she set the home-made volume before John Green, who silently turned the pages, pausing occasionally to caress the images. Returning to the first page he placed his finger under her handwritten text.

'This is a train,' he read, slowly but confidently. Ruth and John Green looked at each other and grinned. Ruth pressed on, determined not to lose momentum. Pointing at a word beginning with 'ch' she asked if John knew what sound those letters made. He did not.

'Choo, choo,' she shrilled, making the motion of a train with her arms. Comprehending, finally, he copied her. He could take the book home to practise, she told him. That night, as she lay in bed, she thought of Anne Of Green Gables and Laura Ingalls Wilder; the girlhood heroines who had inspired her to teach. A smile hovered on her lips as she fell asleep.

***

In the morning she was in the classroom early. As she chalked the date on the blackboard she heard a noise in the playground. John Green, the train book under his arm, was being pursued by a line of his classmates. In unison, they rotated their arms.

'Choo choo! Choo choo! 'they taunted. John Green was a small volcano, set to erupt. The train chugged out of view as the bell rang for the beginning of school.

Having set the class to work, Ruth called John Green to her desk. He swaggered to the front, hands in pockets. Ruth asked where the book was. John Green's lips twitched into a smirk as a hush fell in the room. He jerked his head towards the window. Ruth rose from her chair to look out. Balls of scrunched up sugar paper rolled in the breeze, chased by the seemingly resident dog.

'It was a baby book,' mumbled John Green as the children left their seats and flocked to the window. As she tried in vain to recall them Ruth caught sight of the headmaster peering through the door's glass panel. He strode away down the corridor. Ruth heard the door of his office slam.

Her fingers closed around the wooden ruler on her desk. John Green offered his outstretched palm. The first strike barely tickled his skin. His shoulders shook with suppressed amusement. Ruth tightened her grip. As her second attempt marked the boy's hand she felt a glow of satisfaction. She continued, until John Green shook with fear, not mirth, stopping only when the ruler snapped. The others had returned silently to their places. Ruth would gladly have taken him by the shoulders and shaken the life from him. The bell for assembly called her back. She had lived her whole life governed by bells.

**

Her class, after that, began to march like all the others. Ruth left at the end of the year, to start a family. She would be missed, said the headmaster. She had become a valued member of staff, after a rather shaky start. He winked as he said this.

She never returned to teaching. But in the years that followed she often recalled the terror and the ecstasy of the day she had got the better of John Green. Nothing else in her life ever quite matched it.

Alison Wassell is a former primary school teacher. She volunteers in a charity shop and pays her bills by selling bottled gas part-time in her family's business whilst attempting to become a 'proper' writer. This is the only real ambition she has ever had. She has been longlisted, shortlisted and placed in numerous competitions and published in a handful of anthologies, including Hysteria 1. She has most recently been published in the anthology My Baby Shot Me Down (Blinding Books 2014).

She doesn't really want to be a novelist, and wishes people would have more respect for short stories and flash fiction. She fantasizes about one day earning a living from her writing. Alison shares her home with her cat, Lily, who remains unimpressed by her achievements. When she grows up, she wants to be Alice Munro.

Blog: alisoninwriterland.blogspot.co.uk

Breaking the Surface – Andrea Wotherspoon

'Is this seat taken?' asked a quietly spoken man whom Veronica had never seen before.

'Not at all,' she replied, shifting her chair left, its plastic feet squeaking against the tiled floor. She glanced around the swimming pool cafeteria and was surprised to see that there were no vacant tables. Her table was directly in front of the glass panel which separated the café from the pool, and she had been engrossed in looking for Rachel.

'Very busy this evening, isn't it?' said the man.

'Yes, it's not normally so busy on a Wednesday,' she replied. She lifted her cup and took a sip of lukewarm tea. Every time she came to the pool, she ordered tea which she could never drink. It always seemed to have that sweaty, sweet essence of chlorine. The man sipped tentatively on a hot chocolate. He looked older than Veronica, slim with close cropped greying hair and a hint of stubble, eyes magnified behind round spectacles. She looked away from him and back towards the muffled shouts and splashes from the pool. Where was Rachel? Veronica's heart skipped a beat when she realised she had become distracted from looking for her daughter. Could that be her? Sleek and shiny as a fish, diving in and disappearing below the surface of the water. No, it couldn't be; that girl was too tall. Veronica was never sure. There were so many children in there, all merging into one. The girl's head popped up, dark hair plastered on her head. She reminded Veronica of a seal. It wasn't Rachel.

'Not a swimmer, then?' asked the man. Veronica turned.

'No, definitely a spectator. Although I'm not a fan of the spectating side either, to be honest. The chlorine smell makes me feel quite ill.'

He smiled. 'Same as myself. My daughters are daft on it, though.' He nodded towards the pool. 'Both in there, having a great time. I'm only here as chauffeur.'

Veronica smiled politely and looked back towards the pool. Entering into conversations with people at the pool was difficult. There was so much she couldn't say. It was easier not to talk to people. She just wanted to look for Rachel.

'What about you?' asked the man. Veronica turned back to him.

'Umm, my daughter.' She glanced back towards the pool, to the throng of shrieking, wet people throwing themselves into the water then hauling themselves out again. 'She loves to swim,' she added softly.

'There's my two,' the man said, pointing to two blonde girls. One was sitting on the edge, feet dangling in the green tinged pool, talking to the other girl who bobbed in the water in front of her. 'Heather's the oldest, she's twelve. Jessica's eleven, she's the one in the pool.'

'Right. They look like they're having fun.'

'Oh, no doubt they are,' replied the man with a laugh. 'Is your daughter in there herself, or is she with friends?'

'She's...' Veronica swallowed but saliva caught in her throat and she gasped for breath. Heat overwhelmed her; suddenly she was burning up and could feel her face reddening with each passing second. Just lie, a voice inside her said. Make something up, what does it matter? But for some reason she didn't want to lie to the man.

She tried to lie. She made a show of looking. So many girls, of every age, mixed with boys, mixed with adults. Swimsuits of every colour, everyone blurred as if the water was making their colours run. She looked over where the man's girls had been; they were gone. 'She was there,' Veronica said, frowning, her voice vague. A girl walking along the edge of the pool, her dark hair in tangled fronds. She could be Rachel. A younger looking girl in a pink suit pulling herself out of the pool. Rachel? She sat back, pursing her lips, tears filling her eyes. She should lie to the man, point out any girl. But instead she whispered, 'I can't see her.'

'Oh dear,' the man replied. He momentarily leaned forward as if he were about to spring from his seat, but then he seemed to relax and sat back, elbows on the arms of his chair, hands held in a pyramid in front of him, fingertips touching.

'That might be her,' Veronica mumbled half heartedly. She couldn't look at the man. Her stomach was heavy and she wanted to leave, yet she was rooted to the chair. She reached for her handbag and pulled it on to her lap, desperately scanning the pool for a girl that could be Rachel, so that she could point to her, say ah, there she is and redeem herself in the eyes of this poor man that now probably thought she was insane.

'I actually have three daughters,' the man said. Veronica didn't reply. She was surprised he still wanted to talk to her. 'Ellen's the oldest of the three. She died eleven years ago.'

Veronica's head snapped round, her heart racing. 'I'm so sorry,' she said. The man slowly bowed his head, closing his eyes.

'She would be fourteen now,' he went on. 'She was hit by a car. Heather was in the buggy and Ellen had been holding on to the handle, like she had been taught to. But she spotted someone we knew on the other side of the road, and before I knew it, she was away. The driver wasn't even going that fast, there was nothing he could have done.'

'That's just awful,' Veronica whispered, a hand clasped over her mouth. The heat that had overwhelmed her evaporated just as quickly, and she shivered. Her scalp prickled with goosebumps.

'It was,' the man replied. 'It wasn't easy at the time, I can tell you Especially not with the two younger ones. I blamed myself for a long time but I've made a certain peace with it now. One thing I've learned though, is how to identify other grieving parents. We all grieve differently but the signs are the same.'

It was Veronica's turn to bow her head. The laughing and screaming from the poolside grew louder and the sickly, damp chlorine smell overwhelmed her. She inhaled but her chest was tight. She looked at the cup of tea in front of her, its pale surface blotted with dots of milk, and her stomach turned. Her act was not as good as she had always assumed. This man knew. There was no point in trying to pretend otherwise anymore.

'I know she's dead,' Veronica said. She ran a fingertip through some sticky sugar on the table surface. 'And I know that this is crazy. But we were always here. She came swimming every week, without fail, and I was always here watching her. It was too hard a habit to give up. I know she isn't in there, but I just like sitting here, imagining that she it. Imagining, just for a little while, that everything's ok.' She gave a small laugh. 'I've never spoken to anyone about this before, yet here I am, telling a complete stranger.'

'Sometimes strangers are easier to speak to,' the man replied. 'What happened to Rachel?'

'Here's the irony; she died in a swimming pool. Not this pool, we were away staying with my aunt. Rachel had to have a swim of course. She pestered and pestered me until I took her.' Veronica smiled at the memory, her eyes dry. 'I don't know what happened. She hit her head on the bottom, they think she misjudged the distance. It was different to this pool. I never even noticed until a commotion started, I was too busy reading the paper. Imagine! I always used to watch her, especially when she dived underwater. I would hold my breath until she broke the surface. She was such a strong swimmer yet I always worried. But for some reason, that day, I took it for granted that she would be alright. But...' The words caught in Veronica's throat and she gulped.

The man was shaking his head. 'Not your fault.' His voice was as soft and as soothing to her as cotton wool. 'It was just one of those things. You were doing what you thought was right, and things didn't work out.' He shrugged. 'No ones' fault.'

They sat in silence, looking towards the pool. The man's daughters were engaged in some sort of diving race, lining up beside each other before launching themselves into the water.

'How long ago?' he asked.

She sighed. 'Six months.'

'Not long. It will get easier, I can promise you that. It never goes away, but it does get easier.'

She nodded. 'Thank you.' She pushed the mug of cold tea into the middle of the table then stood up. 'I mean it, thank you.' She smiled at the man, who looked up at her through those round lenses, his eyes wide. He held out his hand.

'Anthony,' he said.

'Veronica,' she replied, shaking his hand.

'You'll be alright?'

'I will.' She smiled again as she shrugged into her jacket, before heading slowly towards the door. She turned just before she left, but his attentions were back on his daughters.

***

It was a cool evening, the air freshened by an earlier shower of rain but the sky was a fading blue and the world looked bright, as if the colours were in sharp focus. There was, she noted, a lightness to her step today. That heavy, leaden feeling that she usually dragged home from the pool was not as heavy as normal. She would be back at the poolside again soon, she knew that. But one Wednesday – soon – she wouldn't go, and that was OK. One day she would break the surface and breathe again.

Andrea Wotherspoon. I'm an economics graduate living by the sea on the north coast of Scotland. I work in waste management by day, and I write fiction in the evenings. I've been writing since my teens but have only recently developed the confidence to start sending my writing out into the world. As well as writing, I love to read, knit, crochet, draw, cook and spend time by the sea. I blog about writing, life, being creative and making ridiculously long lists of stuff at fictionburns.co.uk

The Tears of the Mountain Cherry Tree – Mandy Huggins

As I walk towards the hotel entrance I notice that the sign has been crudely altered with a black marker. The New Hope Motel has become The No Hope Motel; from a fresh start to total despair with the swipe of a pen.

There's certainly no hope of a swim; the empty pool is filled with sunburnt weeds, and the blue tiles are coated with years of highway dust.

I look up at the peeling pink stucco, the rusty railings and the rows of faded doors. I know you are behind one of those doors, and right now I'm pretty nervous. I lick my fingertips and smooth my hair down, then I walk towards the entrance.

A skinny tow-haired boy watches me from the corner, throwing a basketball from one hand to the other. As I walk he starts to bounce the ball, magnifying the tremor of the subway beneath my feet.

I hear music seeping out of the first room I pass; a low-rent clone of Pink Floyd. When I knock on your door, the next one down opens, and a dark haired woman peers out at me. A raven plait falls tangled and thick down her back. She looks like Pocahontas. I nod at her but she turns back inside.

Your door opens a crack and I see one half of a pale face and a shock of ruffled blond hair. You look both wary and surprised, as though I'm the last person you expect or want to see. So much for kidding myself that everything would be ok.

You let me in without a word, staying behind the door, holding it in front of you as a shield. Then you glance furtively at the next room down before coming back inside.

The room smells of unwashed clothes and stale fat. There's a two ring stove in the corner with a dirty frying pan sat atop it, and two neat rows of empty beer cans lined up at the side of the sink.

You stand, hand on hip, in your rumpled sweatshirt, and look me up and down. There are dark rings under your eyes; you look tired, possibly hungover, but there's no sign of anything stronger. And there's no smell of stale cigarettes in here, so I guess you aren't smoking any weed either.

'What do you want, Marnie?' you say at last.

'Who's the spy next door?' I ask, ignoring your question. 'Have you replaced me so quickly? It's only four weeks since you left.'

'What's it to you?'

I shrug, feign disinterest, and pick up a postcard that's propped up on the tiny dining table. I look at the picture and then turn it over without asking, and see your brother's familiar scrawl, dancing untidily across the card like some kind of free form jazz.

'You'd like it here!' it says. 'Great food, great wine, great girls!'

Too many exclamation marks. Too many greats. He protests too much methinks. Sounds like he's not having such a good time after all.

I prop it up against the pepper grinder again, pull out a chair and sit down at the table.

'Any chance of a cup of coffee?' I ask.

You nod and reach for the espresso pot, fill it from the tap and spoon in the coffee. I watch your hand shake as you strike a match for the stove. Then you busy yourself with getting the flame right; turning it up to the highest heat possible without the flames licking up the side. You don't look at me.

I pat the stool next to my chair and announce that I have something to tell you.

You pick up two cups and rinse them out, then you sit down and drum your fingers on the worn formica. I reach out and put my hand over yours to still it. I catch the look in your eyes. The eyes that are still kind. And then I can't speak. I can hear the hiss of the gas, and the faint sound of the music from the room two doors down.

I'm pretty sure you have no idea what I'm going to tell you, but instinctively you know you don't want to hear it, you just want to be left alone to drink yourself into oblivion with the Indian girl next door. The girl who demands nothing, and doesn't try to change you. The girl that you know is safe, because she's so wrong. You know you'll never love her, so she can never hurt you.

You were the boy with the kind eyes, who has become the man I almost destroyed. For ten years I have blamed you for the choice I made when I was seventeen; unfairly, because you never knew I had to make that choice. Somehow you always sensed there was something unspoken between us, and as time passed, the thing grew bigger. So you took revenge for what you didn't understand; with drink and lies, drugs and girls. Until it broke us in two.

You trace your finger along a gouge in the table.

'It's been a rough month, and she's been good to me, you know.'

I assume you mean Pocahontas.

'Pete...'

You look up, meet my gaze just for a moment, then jump up to the stove as the coffee bubbles through. You pick up the cups and pour the strong, dark liquid.

'Milk?'

I shake my head, and you place one of the cups in front of me and sit back down.

'How can you live here?' I say.

We both know you have the money to live somewhere better. It's almost as though you are punishing yourself for giving up on us.

You shrug. 'It suits me,' you say.

This is so much harder than I dreamt it would be. I planned my speech, I wrote it down and practised it in my head. And now I don't know what to do. I hoped that by sharing my news I could save us, but maybe I just want to save myself. Perhaps telling you is the the selfish option.

There is a knock at the door and you scramble to your feet. You only open it a crack and I hear muted voices. I know that is your Indian girl. She has been watching and waiting. She knows that I am still here and she is worried.

I stand up and walk over to the door. You jump as I touch your shoulder, and Pocahontas stares at me with those dark, guarded eyes.

'Don't worry, I'm going. I'd just come to tell Pete that I am leaving town for a while.'

I step past you onto the balcony and walk a couple of steps before I turn and look at you.

'I'll be seeing you around, Pete. Take care of yourself. I'll be in touch...'

I get in my car, but I don't drive away. Once again I have a decision to make. The same decision I had to make ten years ago. But I know I won't make the same choice.

The early autumn breeze blows a shoal of curled pink petals onto the bonnet of my car. Confetti for the end of a marriage. Tears for the end of summer, and for everything lost.

And when I cry, the tears fall like the pink cherry tree blossom outside the war museum.

***

I remember walking through the door of the war museum. Just turned seventeen and fresh with possibilities, life unwinding before me like a bright silken thread. I reached for your hand and looked up into your eyes. They were kind eyes.

For a few minutes I moved around the vast space, glancing at the uniforms in glass cases, looking up at the fragile planes. The bombs unnerved me, even in their benign state; their shape instinctively inspired fear.

I stopped at some photographs. The chilling image of a mushroom cloud, bleak depictions of a barren wasteland, glass bottles melted into deformed shapes. Then I saw the plane. A white bomb with wooden wings. Tiny. A single cherry blossom painted on its side. The face of a pilot. A young face. In his funeral portrait, he stares straight ahead. He had kind eyes.

I squeezed your hand, but I didn't stop reading. The Yamazakura-tai - the Mountain Cherry Blossom Corps. Falling blossoms signifying death in battle. Eyes wide open in the face of the enemy. The battle cry: You and I are cherry blossoms in season. . . Every flower knows it must die. We will die gloriously, then, for our homeland.

When we stepped back out into the sunlight I walked quietly at your side. I knew that I had to tell you. It was there between us; a tangible, solid thing. Tiny, unacknowledged, barely formed.

'Pete,' I whispered.

'Yes?'

You looked down at me, and from your eyes I could see that if I asked, you would do the good, right thing.

We stopped under a tree, heavy with pale blossom. A soft breeze blew petals onto our hair and shoulders. I thought of the pilot with the kind eyes, about to sacrifice his life, and I knew that I couldn't ask you to do the same.

'The museum was sad, wasn't it?' I said, and you brushed my tears away along with the pink petals.

Mandy Huggins loves writing and travel in equal measure, and can often be found gazing into space in airport departure lounges or scribbling in notebooks on trains. Consequently, many of her stories are set in foreign locations, and much of her travel writing involves a morsel of creative fiction – she never encourages the truth to spoil a good story.

Her short fiction and travel pieces have been published online, in anthologies, and in several literary journals, daily newspapers and mainstream magazines. Mandy has also won several writing competitions, and been shortlisted and placed in many others, including those run by New Writer, Lightship Publishing, Fish, Ink Tears and The Telegraph. She was a finalist in the 2013 Bradt/Independent on Sunday

Travel Writing Competition, and recently won the British Guild of Travel Writers New Travel Writer Award 2014.

You can read more of Mandy's work on her blog - troutiemcfishtales.blogspot.co.uk

Sweetie Wife – Clare Archibald

You all told me that hair cannae go white overnight, but mine's did. My colour went; I'm not havering, I know I'm not. I'm here as proof, even if you don't believe it. Well I was here. Och maybe it just seemed like overnight to me. Perhaps I changed really quickly inside but the rest of the world, well ma wee world anyway, only saw me in slow motion.

It keeps happening to me, and I keep on pulling out the white hairs and hiding them in sweetie wrappers, piling them up at the back of the boxbed until I get the chance to bury them in the back green. Digging away with ma trowel like some kind of confused, flapping magpie. Trying to remember the colours of the rainbow and the order they come in. And then I carry on as normal, nobody knows what I'm thinking because I've always got a quiet smile and a friendly ear for everyone. This time I was hoping it'd be different but it's the same except worse. This time though I'm telling you. Did you know I hung down heavy to the floor, my lower half bulging with nature, without nurture. Know that I shuffle around in silence, feeling all the stitches I painstakingly sewed the last time I unravelled? That's me, Saggy Aggie, Droopy Drawers.

Sit by the fire with me, it can be just like those other times, sewing the rags into my underwear, padding my life out with some soft edges to hide in for a bit. Every now and then we'll feel the rhythm of Joe spitting onto the coals, and we can all wonder what he thinks. What he thought would be enough; thoughts can count as feelings can they not? That would do for me. Although the hiss on the coals always eventually comes back as:

"Aggie, should you no be getting the weans tea, rather than sewing a bloody quilt or whitever it is you're faffing about wi?"

I should. It's not their fault after all. I look at the big pan on the range wondering where I get the energy to heave it off and sort the tea. I know that he needs me to wear my pinny like always, and just get on with it.

I'm pinned in my pinny right enough. I never even had a day in bed this time

"Whit's the use in greetin' Aggie? it's life is it no, best just get oan w'i it"

Joe had said, ramming his baccie into his pipe in a way that drew a line under any suffering. Ma grief. I need to make it so that they're the lucky ones, the ones that never knew what it was to go out to the toilet in the back green in the middle of the night and cry enough to create the gas for the lights that weren't there, to sob wide open enough to swallow all the spiders that I tried not to think about round my feet, round my feet and in the ground. Ach I cannae think about the ground that's too much. I spend all day scanning their faces and watching, thinking, wondering what could, what will happen to them? How can we make them lucky? Can you even? A wombful of worries eh?

I pull my pinny straight and replay all the times in my head I've said goodbye to them all already. Just in case something happens. Enough has happened for folk to have an opinion that's for sure. I'm well known down the street, course I am, they will all have had their stuff to say I've no doubt. I heard Mrs. Flanagan say at the back of the Cooperative the other day,

"Aggie's a quiet one, you'd think she had nothing ever happened in her puff '".

I don't reckon you need to shout something from the rooftops to make it real do you? Well, what did Ena know; she was one of life's lucky ones. Och but how can I say that, I'm lucky as well am I not? I've the three living still. Can you compare one woman tae the next, womb tae womb? I never did think so, I know so. I keep myself to myself alright, I've got my own long nights of willing them next door to be fighting again so that my greeting will be met only with the smell of too many families in one outhouse, too many children in one tenement. Too many children.

You wouldnae ever expect the cludgie to be the place where I'd get some comfort. Well not comfort exactly, but relief I suppose. When I take my shot at cleaning it out it feels like a different place than at night. There was one day, the last time, when I was in there cleaning and I found one of my wrappers. I must have dropped it. It made me feel sick to my core to think that I'd lost it and no realised. Found it in the corner all covered wi' the white webbing of a spider. The white hair poking out of the wrapper, looking like it was part of the web, looked after by the spider. I liked that thought, even though they scare me. I swithered over leaving it there with the spider or burying it with the rest. I decided to bury it so they were all the gither.

I crept out that night feeling properly alone even with all the sleeping families cocooning the back green. I caught a glimpse of yon spiders web all lit up by the moon, illuminated like my new head of worries and it made me think I shouldnae be scared of them, they were like me, weaving a web of wool around themselves. I like it out there at night, no-one needing me; wondering about me. Just me and the hairs and now my new friends the spiders. Do you ken that way weans pull the legs off insects sometimes for fun? I never liked that, now I know what it feels like. My legs always feel like they're about to give way on me but I think of ma sweeties and my three and I keep on going. Keep on going.

I'm the net for the three, but I'm bulging with the weight of my catch, wishing them, needing them, to float to the top, away, swimming for their lives. I love to see them run off to the baths their towels tucked into their oxters. And here we are, keeping the heid; me sewing ripped up old towels and sheets into my knickers again. And here I am again losing children like some people lose money down the back of the bus seat.

***

I started a new thing the other day. I tied a few of the white hairs together, it made them look all pretty, like the kind of dancing girls you'd get from cutting shapes out of folded newspaper. I was fair chuffed with that so I double wrapped them; I even used one of the gold foil toffee wrappers I'd been saving for best I suppose. If I'm honest I cried a lot after I threw the soil over them so I think it needs to be a one off, no more dancing girls, or boys for that matter. Afterwards I spun round and round and round in the toilet hoping I'd just pass out and never come back. All that happened though was that I felt sick and stupid, and wanted to cry even more but couldn't catch my breath enough to, like I was drowning in the tears before they even made it out of ma eyes. That night the moon never shone on any webs or on me. It was pitch black when I made my way back up through the close. I could smell the carbolic and it made me feel better, cleaner but also like I was still choking, just silently now. I heaved my body up step after step, thinking how cold the stone would be if I laid down on it, how it might cool and soothe me, like a headstone maybe would. Och that wisnae going to happen, there was hardly enough money for weans that were living never mind dead.

I take a peek into the kitchen to make sure the three are safe and snuggled up the gither in their boxbed. They look like wee characters in a fairy story, all rosy cheeked and peaceful. There was still room for one more in the bed mind you. If they woke up I'd just tell them I was lighting the fire on the range ready to get the stew going for tea that night. If I told anybody what I'd been doing they might no' understand, they might ruin it for me, take it away from me, tell me I'm no right in the head. They widnae understand how beautiful the moon can make white hairs, even white hairs of sorrow. Luminous – that's the word they use all the time in the Mills and Boons books that Ena has a roomful of, got them second hand at Christmas off the woman she cleans for. Me, I don't have the time or money for that, romance real or otherwise, or the right man, I don't suppose, but I love that word. Lit up with light not fumbling around getting in a fankle of darkness. I stub my toe on the dresser as I back out of the kitchen, holding in my pain so as not to wake the wee yins. I look down at the dresser drawer and for a wee minute I see it lit up like a manger with a baby in it. They drawers have done us proud; they've held all kinds – porridge, babies, and sometimes even wee bodies.

I go through to the back room and get in next to Joe, he would never wake up, too tired after a hard day's work at the pit, never missed one in 25 years, never missed me. Even if he had I don't think he'd be anything but annoyed I woke him. I'd never tell him, he's not got white hair, and even if he did and the moon shone on it, so what it wisnae his body that wis bleedin was it.

That's me finished sewing now. Sewing the rag pad to catch the last of my youngest baby. I'm away to the back room now, to put the pad inside my knickers. Then I'm going to look around to see that no-one's watching, get a chair and stand up on it. I'll reach out to behind the back of the wardrobe and pull loose the old biscuit tin I've rammed in there. I'll check that the white hair laid across the top held and down with fancy sellotape is in the right place. I'll take my time to remember every feeling I've had about it. I'll sit and stare myself out in the mirror, brushing and brushing till there's white hairs all over me like I'm a white owl swooping through the night, panicking about not having enough wrappers maybe. Then I think, don't be daft Aggie there's all the wrappers you'll need in here, and that's when I know what I'm going to do. The rainbow I've repeated over and over again as I dig and cover and weep inside has led me here, to this wee pot of gold. Hidden from everybody, just like me, just like them.

***

I'm eating every bit of the sweeties and chocolates hidden inside, stuffing them in me, ramming myself into the tin with every bite until I'm all chewed up nothingness, inside the tin, just a sweetie wife.

Clare Archibald lives on the Fife coast in Scotland with her partner, young daughter and dog. She writes across forms including short stories, poems; stand-up and children's fiction. She is currently writing her first novel, Outwith, and is being mentored to do so by the award winning author Lisa O'Donnell via the Womentoring project.

Clare was picked as an emerging writer to read at Storyshop 2014, the City of Literature showcase at the Edinburgh International Book Festival.

Her last publication was a children's story in Volume 3, Issue 1 of The Looking Glass. Her first story for adults was published in issue 7 of Push with 2 further appearances. She's living in hope for other submissions currently in the ether and in her head.

She recently made a Filmpoem with the artist Gregor McAlpine & the musician/composer Francis Macdonald.

Twitter - Clare Archibald @Archieislander

Advice for Writing Competitions

Competitions are a staple of the writer's life. They provide a punctuation point in the annual calendar and give entrants valuable experience of working to a deadline and with a publisher in many cases. When a writer is shortlisted for inclusion in an a competition anthology it's possible for those who have yet to make the shelves the metaphorical bookstore, to see a little more about how the whole process works, the length of time it takes and the finished product.

But, to be in that happy position there are a number of hoops to jump through first. Not least is entering itself, after all you can't possibly win or even be shortlisted if your masterpiece was never submitted in the first place.

It was with this in mind that I asked judges past and present to put a few thoughts together based on their experience of working with entries to the Hysteria Writing Competition. Their advice is valuable and I would recommend reading it all before making your next attempt in another competition.

Abigail Wyatt – 2014 Judge

I found it hard to think about what advice to give to about entering competitions without harking back to my days as an English teacher and the advice I used to give my pupils before the entered the examination room. If this sounds patronising I apologise in advance but it seems to me that there are a number of useful parallels. 'Read the question carefully', for example becomes 'Make sure you have read the competition guidelines'. I was surprised and saddened by the number of entrants who did not do so and, consequently, fell at the first hurdle.

I would also warn my students against 'showing off' or to 'trying to be clever' and this piece of advice is best translated, I think, as: 'Aim for authenticity and a sense of conviction'. The pieces that stood out for me were those that communicated an emotional and psychological reality. We writers are often exhorted to write about 'what we know' and, in many ways, this is excellent advice. To my mind, however, the very *best* writing is that which takes 'what we know' and presents it to us in a different light, or from an altered perspective, and in so doing, jolts us into seeing and thinking afresh.

Thirdly, I would tell my students: 'Pay attention to detail'. I would remind them that the 'mechanics' of their writing – by which I meant the grammar, the punctuation, the sentence construction, the spelling – were the tools of their trade. I would tell them that there was nothing more important than keeping them polished and well-honed. I still think this is true. Great writers, like great artists, often 'break the rules' but they do so deliberately and, usually, when the rules have first been mastered. It is my firm belief that when we invite a reader to enter into our fictional world then we owe it to them to make every effort in the direction of clarity. If we weary or confuse our readers they are unlikely to come back.

Finally, I would try to impress on my students the importance of originality while, at the same time, warning against the pitfalls of striving for novelty for its own sake. 'Be yourself,' I would tell them, 'but be the very *best* self that you can be'. The most powerful writing, whether in poetry or prose, springs from the heart and soul of the writer. There is an unmistakeable quality to work of this kind that cannot fail to impress.

Abigail Wyatt writes poetry and short fiction from her home near Redruth in Cornwall. She took to writing 'seriously' after a period of illness forced her to give up teaching. Since 2008, her work has been published in more than eighty magazines, journals and anthologies most recently in *Wave Hub: New Poetry from Cornwall* ed. Alan M. Kent (Boutle). She enjoys performance and, together with her partner, singer/songwriter David Rowland, she has appeared at events and festivals throughout the west of Cornwall. She is a Pushcart nominee and a member of the Lapidus organisation. She also the news-based poetry journal *Poetry24*.

Website: abiwyatt.wix.com/abigail-wyatt

Amanda Quinn – 2014 Judge

Thanks for sharing your work with me and congratulations to the winners. My advice is nothing new. I've read it all before and you probably have too. But being a judge reminded me how important the following things are when entering a competition.

Stand out. Write something different. Or differently about something familiar. Think about the other entrants. Who will they be? What will they write about? The judges have hundreds of entries to read in a short amount of time; make sure you catch their attention.

Don't stand out for the wrong reasons. Follow the rules. Use a standard layout and font. Don't let spelling or grammar mistakes distract or annoy the judges. Proofread your piece meticulously. Read it aloud to yourself. How does it sound?

Show don't tell. Let the reader work out what's happening by themselves. Worried you're being too obscure? Ask someone else to read it and tell you what they didn't understand.

And if you're not successful, don't give up. Re-write if you need to and submit somewhere else. Who knows, you may have only just missed out...

Amanda Quinn was born in Birmingham but now lives in the North East. She writes poetry and short fiction. Her work has been published in *Butcher's Dog*, *The Journeyman*, and *Scraps*, the 2013 anthology from National Flash Fiction Day.

You can find her on Twitter: @amandaqwriter.

Sarah Hegarty – 2014 Judge

1. Read, read, read: Whether you want to write flash fiction, stories or poetry – read widely in your chosen genre and you'll absorb its rhythms and structure. All the advice you need is there, from your favourite authors! Just soak it up. And at the same time...

2. Write, write, write: Because writing is like any other activity – the more you practise, the better you get. Set aside time every day, even if it's only ten minutes. Soon you'll find you're writing for longer than you thought you could – and you've got a writing habit.

3. Come up with an original idea: A friend who always seems to win competitions for slogans told me that the first five she thinks up will be the ones everyone else thinks of too. So she keeps going – until she finds something she knows is different. An original idea will make your work leap out at the judges who, you can be sure, will already have read twenty stories on caring for relatives with dementia.

4. Or an original approach: But if you do want to explore a popular topic – because it means something to you, or because you have something new to say – find a different way to do it. Try a different voice, or a different setting.

5. Show don't tell: This is up there with Number 1 – because the more you read, and think about what you're reading, the more you'll see that successful writers leave room for the reader to fill in the gaps. To paraphrase Chekhov: don't tell me Fred's a messy eater – show me the jam on his tie.

6. Re-draft: Hemingway apparently recommended writing drunk and editing sober. Whatever your process, the more time you can leave between bashing out your first draft and coming back to it, the easier it will be to spot clunky sentences, dud descriptions, or a page of throat-clearing before the story starts.

7. Set it out properly: Get the technical stuff right. If you're not sure – and many of us find grammar confusing – there are plenty of writing books and websites with advice. Set out dialogue correctly; set out paragraphs the right way. A great story will shine through sloppy presentation, but daft mistakes make it easy for a judge to rule you out. You wouldn't go to a wedding in your tracky bottoms, would you? Give it your best shot.

8. Check the rules and follow them: Otherwise all your hard work is wasted.

Sarah Hegarty was born in Bristol, and grew up in the north-west. After graduating in Mandarin from Leeds University she worked as a print journalist, latterly as a freelance. She left journalism to start a family and studied for an MA in Creative Writing at Chichester University.

Her short fiction has been published by Cinnamon Press, Mslexia, the Momaya Annual Review and on the web, as well as placed in competitions. Her story *Something Hidden* was the title story of the 2013 Bridge House anthology. Another story, *A Thousand Grains of Sand*, was shortlisted for the 2014 Bridport Prize.

She is working on her second novel, set in the Congo in the early 20th century, the opening of which won the 2014 Yeovil Literary Prize, and was shortlisted for the 2014 Bridport First Novel Award.

Sarah lives in Guildford with her family. You can find out more about her work at sarahhegarty.co.uk, and follow her on Twitter @SarahHegarty1

Sophie Duffy – 2014 Judge

Write a proper story. Don't write a 'nice' piece of writing or an 'amusing' anecdote. Something has to happen. There has to be a reason for the reader to invest their time in your story. What is the payoff?

Know the difference between flash and poetry. That means read lots of both and write lots of both.

Enter the right piece for the right competition. Do your homework. Check out last year's winners and shortlist and get a feel for the type of writing and story that has risen to the top.

Keep your eyes on the prize. Decide if the potential rewards are worth a punt, not just in financial return but in terms of your writing career. Maybe the cash prizes are small but the winning stories will be published in an anthology. This is a great way to get published and to add to your CV. (Do check the contract.)

Follow the rules! You'll be disqualified if you don't and then you've wasted not only your money but your chance of winning.

Develop that hard skin. As soon as you receive a rejection, try and work out why the piece was rejected and revise it for another competition. Don't take it personally. I once entered a competition and didn't even get long listed. I sent it straight back out to another competition and it came second. One judge's taste can vary hugely from another's. Or maybe I just found the right competition for my work.

Keep sending out stuff. As long as you have something out there, you have a chance of winning something. If it stays in your drawer or on your laptop then it has no chance. Speculate to accumulate.

Sophie Duffy is the author of two novels both published by Legend Press. *The Generation Game* won the Yeovil Literary Prize and the Luke Bitmead Bursary and *This Holey Life* was runner up in the Harry Bowling

Prize. She is part of Creative Writing Matters which runs writing workshops and courses, offers manuscript appraisals and mentoring, and administers writing competitions including the Exeter Novel Prize. She lives in Teignmouth, Devon, with her husband, three teenagers and two Tibetan Terriers.

You can find her on: sophieduffy.com, creativewritingmatters.co.uk and sophieduffy.wordpress.com

Tracy Fells – 2014 Judge

Tracy lives close to the South Downs in West Sussex. She has won and been placed in numerous competitions for fiction and drama. Her short stories and flash fiction are published online and in anthologies. She was shortlisted for the 2014 Commonwealth Writers Short Story Prize and is a finalist in the WriteIdea 2014 Prize. Currently she is working on a novel and an MA in Creative Writing at Chichester University. Tracy shares a blog with The Literary Pig (tracyfells.blogspot.co.uk/) and tweets as @theliterarypig.

And here are some thoughts/tips on writing competitions:

It goes without saying, or I hope it does, that if you enter any writing competition then ensure you've read, understood and followed all the rules and conditions. Otherwise, you literally are throwing away an entry fee.

Reading all the entries for the 2014 Hysteria competition was a pleasurable challenge, but at times I'm sure I shouted at my laptop in frustration because a common problem in all categories was "the ending".

Quite a number of well-written pieces, both prose and poetry, were let down by the writer not following through and giving the reader a satisfactory conclusion. The story/poem started brilliantly, hooked me right in, continued with an intriguing narrative or idea, but then suddenly it was all over. Sometimes I even wondered if the ending had been missed off by mistake – had the writer forgotten to send that final critical page?

Use the word count and take your reader right to the end of the story's narrative arc. Please don't leave them dangling. Wanting a story to go on is natural, but an ending where the key questions are still unanswered or even worse forgotten is torture for a reader. So my plea for any writers entering competitions is: please think of the reader in the writing process, give them the full experience, show off your writing skills and give them a piece with a beginning, middle and ending.

Veronica Bright – 2014 Judge

Have you ever seen someone hopping round the kitchen in excitement, like an overstimulated frog? Have you ever been that person? If you've won a prize – especially one you've worked indescribably hard to win - I bet you can empathise with a sudden burst of unrestrained joy like this. Amphibians apart, one thing is true. Your story or poem won't win a competition unless you take a deep breath and enter it.

Entering competitions is fun. Yes, really. They focus the mind, and because there's a deadline, even the fussiest perfectionist can't go on editing forever.

TIPS FOR SUCCESS: FIRST THE OBVIOUS

- Read the rules and obey them. If they say Times New Roman 12, then that's what they want.
- Do not put your name on the entry itself.
- Do not exceed the word count.
- Get your entry in by the closing date.

OK. So far so good. Now comes the tricky bit.

WHAT TO WRITE ABOUT

Some competitions give you a theme or subject. It's worth thinking carefully about what you are going to write. Brainstorm your ideas. Mutter on the bus if you have to. Just remember, there may be a hundred or more people entering this one, and if you can come up with a truly sizzling plot, so much the better.

Other competitions give you a free reign. Style, plot, and characters are left entirely up to you. This gives you the chance to write your own unique poem or story. And when you focus on making that piece of work the best it can possibly be, you'll find you improve as a writer.

IN WITH A CHANCE: THE WOW FACTOR

- Use creative language that captures the judge's imagination. Make him/her say, 'I wish I'd thought of that.'
- Once your entry is written, read it aloud. This way you can hear whether it sounds right, or whether it needs tweaking a bit. It might help to ask a friend or family member to read it too. Ask them for constructive criticism. Is anything confusing? Is there anything that needs changing? You don't have to do what they suggest, but their opinion is worth considering.
- Read winning entries in a range of competitions - online or in anthologies. Why was this particular poem judged so highly? Why did that story catch the judge's eye?
- If you don't make the winning list this time, could your entry be improved and then entered into another competition?

DON'T GIVE UP. BELIEVE IN YOURSELF

Go on - give yourself a challenge. Enter a competition. And while you wait for the result…. enter another one. And who knows, you may be "doing the frog" around your own kitchen in a few months' time.

Veronica Bright won the Woman and Home short story competition in 2005, and since then she has won a string of prizes for her short stories, and her work has appeared in numerous anthologies. While she was teaching, Veronica wrote two non-fiction books for KS1 teachers – *Frogs in Assembly* and *Robots in Assembly* (both published by Kevin Mayhew, Ltd). Now retired, she has embraced a new life as a writer and local speaker. She is trying to find a home for her children's novel, and is working on her first novel for adults. Veronica runs the Plymouth Christian Writers, and is also a member of the Plymouth Writers Group. She appreciates the peace and quiet now that her children have grown up and left home, but welcomes interruptions that involve tea and chocolate biscuits. Website: veronicabright.co.uk

Anne Wilson – 2013 Judge

Ask yourself a few questions, weigh the odds:

Why this competition? Do you just want to test yourself, build your confidence as a writer, or do you seriously believe that this is the competition in which you stand a good chance of success - in which case:-

Are you good with disappointment/rejection? If the answer to this question is 'no', then this coping mechanism needs more work experience anyway.

Do you have your eye on a prize? Most comps ask for a fee and this amount can vary quite a bit making it a good idea to look at the fee-to-prize ratio and estimate whether this is a relatively small competition attracting a modest number of entries or one advertised internationally and expecting a deluge.

Are you aware that many comps retain the right to publish all short-listed stories? Or perhaps this comp is run to produce a charity anthology and is more than welcome to publish your work.

Have you read about the judges of your chosen comp and also read the work of previous winners? Well run comps usually make this information available.

Have you checked how many weeks/months for which the organisers might hold your story in suspended animation during which time protocol prefers you not to send it elsewhere. Finally, never unwittingly give away your copyright.

Your entry:

Originality. Is your story original? No plot is truly original but have you found a new twist?

First paragraph. You want to encourage the reader to read on. A full-blown shock isn't necessary but aim for mystery, a question posed or a note of intrigue, something which makes the reader wonder what happens, where things go from here. Embed a narrative hook.

Language. Keep it tight. No clichés, cut down on adverbs, wherever possible axe your 'ings'. Metaphors are good, and use your thesaurus; have you really used the best word to convey your meaning? You know all this stuff, you're a writer.

Emotion. Try to make the reader care about your characters. How your reader responds to them begins with their name. Make them real with the way they speak, what they wear, their individual quirks and mannerisms. Think what emotion you want this character to make your reader feel. Try to remember the golden rule of 'show don't tell'.

Structure. Very important. Your story needs to have some kind of arc of beginning, middle and end. It should close leaving the reader satisfied with the outcome, and not feeling you have left something out or could have put more in.

Presentation. First impressions count and you want your work to be taken seriously. Look at punctuation, layout and basic grammar; please try your hardest.

I grew up in the north-west of England around the Morecambe Bay area and have always filled my free time with my favourite hobbies of reading and writing.

I also lived for a number of years on the Balearic Island of Mallorca which inspired my first novel, *Here Be Dragons: A Tale of Mortals, Myths and Mystery*, set in Mallorca and Denmark. I have a journal-blog on my website telling the story of these ex-pat years.

On my return to the UK, I was employed by my Local Education Authority to deliver the Additional Literacy Support programme to under-achieving junior groups and subsequently ran both literacy and art workshops.

In 2010 I gained a BA (Hons) in Advanced Creative Writing through the Open University. My short fiction has since appeared in a number of anthologies, most recent of which is *Light in the Dark*, a compilation of short stories for Christmas, available in November from Bridge House Publishing. I have two current projects, another novel entitled *A Bundle of Bones* and a sequel to *Here be Dragons*, as yet untitled.

Penny Laurence –2013 Judge

1. Make sure the competition is for you - read other work that's won previous competitions - is it reminiscent of your writing or totally not your style. Chances are you'll have better luck in a comp that already likes the kind of things you do.
2. Research the judges. Find out who they are and read what they write. Again, if their style is like yours, chances are you'll have a better chance of winning than if it's the polar opposite.
3. Read the rules and follow them - many competitions are judged blind, so making the mistake of leaving your name on the file may get you disqualified before they even read a word, others won't accept attachments, or files that aren't double spaced or in Times New Roman etc. Whatever the rule is, follow it. You don't want to annoy someone who's judging your work or worse knock yourself out for a silly mistake.

Penelope Laurence got her start in writing in the story room for the TV soap Neighbours. For more than a decade she has written and edited kids television, soap, animation, TV movies and documentary series in both Australia and Canada, including for the Australian Logie Award winning series "H2O: Just Add Water".

In addition to her work in television, Penelope is an experienced travel journalist with articles appearing in Lonely Planet and newspapers such as The Australian, The Age and The Toronto Star.

Her short fiction has been published in the American anthology Just Like A Girl; A Manifesta and the British anthology, Hysteria1. Currently she lives in Montreal, Canada with her whippet, Keating.

Ruby Cowling – 2013 Judge

It's always said, but it's worth repeating: the judging of story and poetry competitions is subjective. Just as you may love a particular book, while your friend hated it, readers are people and all judges are different.

This means two things: that there's nothing *guaranteed* to get your story or poem to the top, but also that you shouldn't be too dejected if it doesn't. I've had stories suddenly do well in one competition after getting nowhere in several others. So do get your work out to as many appropriate places as you can, because you never know when someone who's on your wavelength will happen to be reading for that competition.

That said, notice the phrase "appropriate places". RESEARCH is time well spent. Research both the publication – if the competition's being run by, say, a magazine – and the judges, if they're known. What sort of thing has appeared in that magazine? Do they like a lighter tone, or something more literary? Get hold of previous years' winning entries and read them. Read what the judges (who are usually writers) write. Do they obviously love a strong, suspenseful storyline? Is beautiful language clearly their thing? Do they reveal a twisted sense of humour you can appeal to?

Obviously, the story or poem itself needs to be "good". And "good" is still, to an extent, subjective. However, if:

a) we know what the story or poem is "about",
b) we work at it, through many drafts, including reading it out loud to ourselves,
c) we know why every sentence is there, what work it's doing,
d) we've got past both "it's genius" and "it's terrible" to "I've made it the best it can be",
e) there's a good chance it's good enough.

Double-check the competition's specific rules, such as word or line count maximums. Sometimes a particular font and line spacing is specified. (It might seem unnecessary, but clarity and uniformity makes it much easier for readers to get through dozens of entries without a headache. And you don't want your piece to be the one that brings on the headache.)

Check anonymity rules: more often than not, you'll have to completely remove all identifying information from the main document. This can instantly disqualify you, so make extra-sure.

Get someone else to check for errors. Typos really throw the reader out of a story – and can completely derail a poem. Best to get rid. Also, a fresh reader will spot inconsistencies such as Friday night becoming Thursday morning, or a character taking off her coat twice.

This is all work, but it's worth it.

But the most important advice is to keep at it. The more you read and write, the better you get, and if you keep entering competitions carefully, conscientiously and, well, copiously, one day you'll win one. Think of that!

About The Hysterectomy Association

The Hysterectomy Association provides impartial, timely and appropriate information and support to women. It was founded in the mid 1990's by Linda Parkinson-Hardman who is the author of several books about hysterectomy, online business and one novel.

It is based in Dorset in the UK and you can find out more about the association through the following accounts:

Website: hysterectomy-association.org.uk
Facebook: facebook.com/HysterectomyUK
Twitter: @HysterectomyUK
LinkedIn: linkedin.com/company/the-hysterectomy-association

Other books from The Hysterectomy Association include:

- 101 Handy Hints for a Happy Hysterectomy
- In My Own Words: Women's Experience of Hysterectomy
- Losing the Woman Within
- The Pocket Guide to Hysterectomy
- A Diva's Guide to the Menopause - Short Story
- Hysteria Anthologies

You can connect directly with Linda at womanontheedgeofreality.com.